A sly, sexy grin
mouth. "You do

"Not one bit."

She batted her eyes. "Oh, Russell. Flattery will get you everywhere."

At that, he had to laugh. "You're a piece of work. I'm glad I saved your life today."

She picked up a pen and threw it at him. "No fair bringing the whole saving-my-life thing into it."

The pen hit him in the chest and he snatched it up. Mont Blanc. For what that sucker cost, she shouldn't be throwing it around.

"I'll make you a deal. You don't try to play me and I won't remind you I saved your life." He held out his hand. "Deal?"

She glanced at his hand and pursed her lips.

After what felt like another solid minute, she reached her hand out. "Fine. Deal."

Russell didn't know if it was the thrill of having her agree or just the touch of her hand, but he was suddenly reluctant to let go.

THE DEFENDER

USA TODAY Bestselling Author

ADRIENNE GIORDANO

LONDON PUBLIC LIBRARY

If you purchased this book without a cover you should be aware that this book is stolen property. It was reported as "unsold and destroyed" to the publisher, and neither the author nor the publisher has received any payment for this "stripped book."

Recycling programs
for this product may
not exist in your area.

ISBN-13: 978-0-373-69769-4

THE DEFENDER

Copyright © 2014 by Adrienne Giordano

All rights reserved. Except for use in any review, the reproduction or utilization of this work in whole or in part in any form by any electronic, mechanical or other means, now known or hereafter invented, including xerography, photocopying and recording, or in any information storage or retrieval system, is forbidden without the written permission of the publisher, Harlequin Enterprises Limited, 225 Duncan Mill Road, Don Mills, Ontario M3B 3K9, Canada.

This is a work of fiction. Names, characters, places and incidents are either the product of the author's imagination or are used fictitiously, and any resemblance to actual persons, living or dead, business establishments, events or locales is entirely coincidental.

This edition published by arrangement with Harlequin Books S.A.

For questions and comments about the quality of this book, please contact us at CustomerService@Harlequin.com.

® and TM are trademarks of Harlequin Enterprises Limited or its corporate affiliates. Trademarks indicated with ® are registered in the United States Patent and Trademark Office, the Canadian Trade Marks Office and in other countries.

Printed in U.S.A.

ABOUT THE AUTHOR

USA TODAY bestselling author Adrienne Giordano writes romantic suspense and mystery. She is a Jersey girl at heart, but now lives in the Midwest with her workaholic husband, sports-obsessed son and Buddy the Wheaten Terrorist (Terrier). She is a cofounder of Romance University blog and Lady Jane's Salon-Naperville, a reading series dedicated to romantic fiction.

Please visit www.adriennegiordano.com. Adrienne can also be found on Facebook, at www.facebook.com/AdrienneGiordano Author, and on Twitter, at www.twitter.com/AdriennGiordano. For information on Adrienne's street team, Dangerous Darlings, go to www.facebook.com/groups/DangerousDarlings.

Books by Adrienne Giordano

HARLEQUIN INTRIGUE

1483—THE PROSECUTOR
1502—THE DEFENDER

CAST OF CHARACTERS

Penny Hennings—Sassy Chicago defense attorney determined to build a name for herself and step out of her hotshot father's shadow.

Special Agent Russell "Russ" Voight—Determined FBI agent who will stop at nothing to crack the massive financial fraud case he's been working for over a year.

Gerald Hennings—Senior partner from Hennings and Solomon who is known in Chicago for winning unwinnable cases. Also Zac and Penny's father.

Zac Hennings—Assistant state's attorney in Chicago and the beloved brother of Penny Hennings.

Colin Heath—Con artist being investigated by the FBI for financial fraud.

Brent Thompson—Deputy U.S. marshal assigned to protect Penny after threats are made against her.

Chapter One

Standing on the Cook County Federal Courthouse steps, special agent Russ Voight decided Penny Hennings deserved a star on the Perfect Posteriors of America wall of fame.

Maybe that was sexist, but since his meeting with Penny had been put on ice while she and Gerald Hennings—her legendary defense-attorney father—held an impromptu press conference, Russ needed a way to distract himself. And Penny's rear provided a great distraction.

Months ago, his coworkers at the Chicago FBI field office had dubbed her Killer Cupcake for her aggressive cross-examination skills, but to Russ's way of thinking, she might be Killer Cupcake for other reasons. Those reasons having nothing to do with a courtroom and everything to do with her, his bedroom and lots of free time.

Ah, distractions. How he loved them.

Bang. A gunshot cracked the air.

Gerald ducked. Penny didn't. Blood roared to the front of Russ's brain. He snatched his sidearm from his holster, pushed off the iron railing he'd been leaning on and spotted Penny—not ten feet away—frozen on the steps as the reporter in front of her crumpled. *Hit.*

Loud, ear-blasting screams erupted. Pedestrians dived to the ground—dead-last thing they should do—or ran like hell, *exactly* what they should do. Russ sprinted toward

Penny, still glued to her spot, and did a quick recon. *Where's the shooter?*

Bang.

Across the street. High up.

"Run!" Russ shouted.

But Penny didn't move. She just stood there in the streaming sunshine while her red power suit made one hell of an amazing target. One step below, her father had dropped. Whether he'd been hit or not, Russ couldn't tell. *Get there.* Three more steps. He latched on to Penny's arm, dragging her behind him. Gerald Hennings lifted his head. *Alive.* "Move!"

Penny turned back to her father. "Dad."

"You've got to move," Russ yelled.

But Penny dug in, yanking free to go to her father. "I can't leave him."

Bang.

Another shot pierced the step next to Gerald and a hunk of cement flew.

Penny's perfect porcelain skin went white. Game over. If he didn't do something, she'd be dead on the next shot.

His brain in full overload, he plowed into her, wrapping his hand around the back of her head to break the landing. They hit the cement and a rush of air exploded from his lungs.

"Oofff," Penny said.

Bang.

Right side. *Find the shooter.* With Penny trapped under him, he lifted his head an inch and glanced across the street. Parking garage.

The shooter had to be on one of the top floors of the parking garage.

Onlookers continued to scatter, their shouts clanging together. From the courthouse doors, armed guards charged out, weapons drawn. Pedestrians on the sidewalk had either fled or taken cover. Some huddled behind trees or garbage cans or any other solid object.

Gerald was still sprawled beside them. He faced Russ and Penny, and his blue eyes were loaded with fear that Russ had seen too many times. *We've got to move.*

Suddenly, the air went still and Russ lifted his head another inch. A slight wind rustled leaves and the bright blue of a May sky taunted him, because some psycho decided today would be the day to go stone-cold crazy on a bunch of civilians.

Under him, Penny moved. *Now* she wanted to move?

"Stay down."

Keeping low, she reached for her father's hand. "Daddy?"

"I'm okay," he said.

She shifted again and Russ pressed his body weight into her. On the middle of the expansive and now-empty courthouse steps, right beside a wounded reporter, they were a beautifully open target.

He swung his head, searching for anything that would provide cover. Nothing. Not one damn thing. Run. They'd have to risk it and hope one of them didn't get popped. Below them, the woman who'd been hit whimpered. He needed to get her out, too.

"Hang in there," he yelled. "We'll get you to a hospital."

Having no idea how badly she was injured, he didn't know if she could even understand him.

Sirens blared as Chicago P.D. cruisers stormed the area. "Parking garage!" he hollered at what looked like a detective jumping out of an unmarked car. "High floor. Right side." He went back to Penny still under him. "Are you hit?"

She lifted her head. "I don't think so. But something is poking my butt."

A punch of relief ripped into him. Damn, she'd scared him by freezing up like that. He eased her head back to the ground, hoping she'd forget about the thing poking her.

An armored BearCat screamed to the curb and SWAT

guys funneled out, loaded with combat gear, ready for battle.
"Shooter in the garage!" Russ yelled.

Someone save us. Someone save us. Someone save us.

Penny's pounding head would not let up. Over and over the screams and the crack of shots and the sirens replayed in her mind, the sounds pummeling her, making fear a ripe sting against her body. She closed her eyes. *One second.* To focus.

Now that she knew her father was alive, they'd figure out a way to safety. With an FBI agent on top of her, they'd manage a plan.

The pounding eased a fraction and she opened her eyes. Just below her, Dad stared at her, his face stacked with terror she didn't know her warrior father could feel.

"Russell, we need to move."

"No kidding, Penny. Give me a sec."

She rolled her eyes. Alphas. Always needing to be in charge.

"What's…what's poking me? Could I have gotten hit?"

"The parking garage," he hollered at the SWAT team.

He waved his right arm and the bit of movement increased the pressure on her butt. *What the heck?* "Russell, I think I'm hit."

"I don't think you're hit."

"Then what's that damned poking?"

"Uh, sorry," he said. "That's, uh…ah, cripes…it's…me. It happens sometimes. Adrenaline."

What? She focused on Russ's body, the weight of it, the location of their various body parts and— *Oh, stop it.*

Men.

"You have an *erection?*" she muttered, hoping her father wouldn't hear. *"Now?"*

"Hey, it's involuntary."

Some nut was shooting at them and the FBI agent, the

one who had just saved her life, had an erection. Unbelievable. "Well, get. It. *Off.*"

"Penny," her father said, "quiet."

She'd never understand men. Never. She didn't understand a lot of things right now. All she and her father were doing was talking to reporters, trying to get a sound bite for their client, and suddenly everything exploded. Instead of herding her father to safety, she'd stood there, lost in the paralyzing fear of her thoughts, a wimpy girl, not knowing what to do. Pathetic. Truly pathetic.

And Russell Voight, a man who normally sparked all kinds of fantasies in her mind, on top of her with a giant—really giant—erection, wasn't helping her current state of confusion.

"It's okay," Russ said to her father. "She's scared. People babble."

"I don't babble."

"Yeah, you do. On three, we're all bolting to the building. Stay low. And get rid of those heels. You need to haul."

She nodded, kicked off her spiked heels and touched her father's shoulder. "Are you ready?"

"Yes."

"We're good, then," Russ said. "One, two, three."

He jumped up and the sight of all that quick movement stunned her. He squeezed her hand with enough force that a knuckle popped, and then he dragged her to her feet and sprinted toward the building. Wait. *Dad.* Penny glanced behind her, spotted her father a foot behind and reached back for him.

"Go, Penny. I'm fine."

The safety of the lobby was just ahead and Penny stared at the back of Russ's head, focused on all that thick dark hair because the man had amazing hair and it was so much better than thinking about gunfire.

He swung open the lobby door and shoved her through. "Find an interior room and stay there. I'll find you."

"Russell!"

"Go. I'll find you. I have to help out here."

Chapter Two

Three hours later, after helping secure the crime scene, Russ rode the elevator to the tenth floor of the swanky downtown building where Hennings & Solomon was housed. Penny had already been questioned by investigators at the scene, but for some reason—who was he kidding? he knew the reason—he needed to put eyes on her. The woman's aggressive defense-lawyer attitude and sharp tongue drove him insane, but deep down, when confronted with his baser needs, he had an itch for her.

So, yeah, apparently he was a sick, demented freak, because Penny Hennings was a viper. Five months ago, she'd murdered him on a cross-examination that left him exhausted, frustrated and with a battered ego. Thus, the Killer Cupcake moniker. Without a doubt, she was a looker. Blond hair, blue eyes and a face so perfect he wanted to run his fingers over it just to say he'd done it. *Easy, boy.* At first look, her petite size fooled people, but that mouth made up for anything she lacked in stature. Russ watched the numbers on the elevator blink off and he laughed.

Sick, demented man.

The elevator door slid open and he was greeted by a thickly carpeted waiting area, where the typical hot, young receptionist cooed into her headset, "Hennings and Solomon, how may I help you?"

You can get off the phone and point me to Penny. Russ

waited. It was well after five, but the receptionist remained at her post fielding calls, probably press people wanting a statement about the shooting. Everyone wanted a statement.

Already tired of waiting, he badged the receptionist, who put her calls on hold to direct him to Penny. Nothing like an FBI badge to get someone's attention.

Having never been at this office, Russ counted down the doors and glanced at nameplates as he strode by. Most of the doors were closed, but a few remained open. The occupants glanced up at him, noting his rumpled navy suit and the unbuttoned shirt collar. After the day he'd had, the FBI would have to deal with his loose tie.

Two open doors stood at the end of the long corridor. Penny's, the receptionist had told him, would be the second one from the end, and as he drew closer, the long hallway suddenly echoed with the sound of her voice.

"No," she said. "I'll bring him in. I'm not letting you guys parade my client in front of a bunch of news cameras. He's a businessman, for crying out loud. Get over it."

Even after getting shot at, she continued to do her job. Viper status aside, he admired that. *Sick, demented man.* He wasn't the only one, because the poor schmuck on the other end of Penny's phone call obviously didn't realize he wouldn't win.

Russ paused outside the half-open door. Not to listen, but to get his head together and organize his thoughts and emotions. To shake off the exhaustion sitting on him like solid cement. What a damned day.

Penny had almost gotten blown away. If one of those rounds had connected, that pretty head of hers would have disintegrated. *Poof!*

Gone.

Incinerating heat zinged up the back of his neck. He couldn't be emotional about her. Not when it might give her, the lawyer defending a woman who could be a key witness in his multimillion-dollar fraud case, the upper hand.

"Fine," Penny said. "Get back to me. I can have him down there tomorrow. No perp walk. He'll just quietly turn himself in."

A smack—the phone hitting the base—came from inside the office.

"Idiot," she muttered.

He knocked lightly and pushed open the door. "Hey, I saved your life today. Don't call me an idiot."

Shockingly enough, those perfect bow lips eased into a smile. "Not you. *Idiot.*"

Russ grinned and stepped inside the office. She sat back, rested her head against the cushion. Her perfume, something light and fresh, not flowery or overpowering, hung in the air and he tried to place it. *No idea.* He liked it, though. Reminded him how much he loved a woman's scent.

Her red suit jacket—that blazing target that almost got her killed—hung on the back of the chair and she'd pushed up the sleeves of her white blouse. A few strands of long blond hair had busted free of her hair clip and hung down the sides of her drawn face. The look suited her, gave her an edgy, just-rolled-out-of-bed appearance, and Russ decided thinking about Penny and a bed at the same time could get a man in trouble.

He dropped into the fancy leather guest chair in front of her desk. "You okay? Relatively speaking."

"I'm not in the morgue, so I guess I'm okay."

"Scary as hell."

She rolled her lips together and breathed deep. "I froze. How ridiculous."

After what she'd been through, she questioned her reaction? Killer Cupcake didn't just shred witnesses—she shredded herself. "You were terrified. I've seen seasoned agents react like that. Don't think too hard on it."

"How's the reporter?"

"Still in surgery."

"That poor woman. And the shooter? Did they find him yet?"

Russ shook his head. "No. The crime-scene guys are on it. We'll find him."

"You think so?"

"I'd be a crummy FBI agent if I didn't."

She shrugged.

"How's your dad?"

"Rattled, but fine. My brother came by and we double-teamed him. Forced him out the door."

She stared straight ahead, blinked a couple of times—*uh-oh*—and slapped one hand across her eyes. Damn, he didn't want to see Killer Cupcake cry. He resented the hell out of it that some psycho reduced this fiery woman to tears. "Penny—"

She held her other hand up and Russ stopped talking. Finally, she slid her hand away and focused on him with an intensity that had him shifting in his seat. He'd seen that look five months ago from the witness stand.

"I'm sorry, Russell. I almost got you killed today."

Not what he'd expected. Score one for her on the surprise attack. "That's not on you. You were standing on the steps. How is it your fault some nut decided shooting innocent civilians would solve his problems? Whatever the hell they are."

"But—"

"Penny. Stop."

She closed her mouth. No. Really? If he'd known it was that easy to keep her quiet, he'd have done it months ago.

She threw her hands up. "*Russell,* I was trying to take responsibility for my actions."

There we go. Much better. *Killer Cupcake returns.* "I don't want to hear you apologize. Not for this." He grinned, shifted forward and focused on those hot blue eyes of hers.

"If you want to apologize for something, apologize for beating the hell out of me in court five months ago. My ego still hasn't recovered."

She scoffed, "Never. Besides, that was an excellent cross. Probably my best work."

"Congratulations. I was the victim."

She scooted forward in her chair, her smile drifting wide. "You held your own. As I recall, you rather enjoyed the battle."

Some truth there. Maybe he would have enjoyed it more had he not been the guy in the witness box, but in a seriously twisted way, he got off watching her stalk around the courtroom, hurling impossible, well-developed questions at him.

"You're tough, Penny, but I'm not afraid of you."

"Too bad. I suppose."

He cracked up—couldn't help it. Wanting this woman was a death wish. Simple as that. Also a damned shame, because he couldn't have her. Not when her job required her to dismantle months—sometimes years—of work that guys like him busted their tails on. He wholeheartedly believed every American deserved a fair trial, but at the end of some seriously rotten days, he wondered how defense lawyers justified getting murderers off.

"Anyway," she said. "Why are you here? More questions?"

"No. We never had our meeting from this afternoon."

Before the shooting, they were scheduled to meet after her court appearance to discuss a deal for a witness Russ needed on a stock-fraud case.

In one smooth motion, Penny bolted straight and threw her shoulders back. Battle mode. "Elizabeth Brooks. You still want to discuss it after today?"

"If you're up for it."

Penny cocked one of her perfect eyebrows. "Oh, Russell, I'm always up for it."

Didn't that get him thinking about things he shouldn't

be thinking? Things like Penny Hennings sprawled naked in his bedsheets. *Sick, demented man.* And what was up with the *Russell* business. She always called him by his full name when everyone else called him Russ. Or various other four-letter words.

He smacked his hand on his armrest. "Then let's do it."

"You're on. Elizabeth is willing to testify, but she'll need protection."

"She'll give me everything?"

Penny nodded. "All she knows."

As defense lawyers went, Penny Hennings was as smart and slick as they came. Worse, she was beautiful and knew how to manipulate men. An all-around excellent package. Had she not earned a living trying to decimate his cases, he could probably love her. But if he gave her even the slightest edge, she'd gut him.

A sly, sexy grin spread over Penny's mouth. "You don't trust me?"

"Not one bit."

She batted her eyes. "Oh, Russell. Flattery will get you everywhere."

At that, he had to laugh. "You're a piece of work. I'm glad I saved your life today."

She picked up a pen and threw it at him. "No fair bringing the whole saving-my-life thing into it."

The pen hit him in the chest and he snatched it up. Montblanc. For what that sucker cost, she shouldn't be throwing it around. He set it back on the desk. "I'll make you a deal. You don't try to play me and I won't remind you I saved your life." He held out his hand. "Deal?"

If she agreed to this it would be the second miracle of the day. The first being that no one died in that hellacious shooting on the courthouse steps. She glanced at his hand and pursed her lips.

Russ dropped his hand. "You're afraid you can't do it."

"Oh, please!"

So damned hot.

After what felt like another solid minute, she reached her hand out. "Fine. Deal."

The handshake was nothing and everything he expected. Penny had a firm grip, but her hand was small and delicate and smooth, and he took a second to consider other delicate and smooth areas he'd like to touch.

Hokay. Rough day. Clearly, lascivious thoughts were a coping strategy. Russ cleared his throat.

Penny got up and asked, "Are you okay? Let me get you water."

What he really needed was a Scotch. She strode to the minifridge in the corner and Russ's gaze shot to her feet, where she'd lost the crazy heels she'd been wearing earlier. Now he wasn't sure which was more of a turn-on: Penny in heels or Penny in bare feet. Either way, he had no argument.

She handed him a water bottle, then took the seat next to him. Interesting, that. Some women would stay behind the desk to remind him that (a) he was the guest and (b) she had control.

And suddenly, much to his consternation, he liked Penny Hennings a whole lot more.

Russ slammed half the water bottle—could really use a Scotch—and replaced the lid. "Elizabeth Brooks. I want everything on Heath and her involvement in the pump-and-dump scheme."

The woman in question was the widow of a stockbroker involved in a hundred-million-dollar fraud scheme. The broker and his partner, Colin Heath, created shell companies and then issued the stock for themselves. They publicized how great their companies were through press releases, industry newsletters and any other form of communication they could find. When their victims went crazy buying their stock, thereby pumping up the price, the broker and Heath dumped their shares and made a killing. They also bankrupted thousands of innocent investors.

When the broker decided he'd had enough of screwing people out of their life savings, Colin Heath arranged for him to have a timely and torturous death. It was a murder carried out by Heath's number-two guy, a real leg-breaker who'd been dumb enough to get caught. Only the guy wasn't talking and the FBI didn't have enough to nail Heath.

Nailing Heath was what Russ wanted. And apparently what Elizabeth Brooks, via Penny, could give him.

"She'll talk," Penny said. "She needs immunity. And protection."

"Why is she suddenly willing to talk? Her husband's been dead for months."

Penny hesitated. Already their deal crumbled. Russ stood, set the water bottle on Penny's desk, more than ready to walk away. He wanted Colin Heath, but Penny wouldn't play him.

He took one step and she tugged on the back of his jacket. "Don't go. I was thinking. That's all."

Turning back, Russ stared down at her, took in those amazing blue eyes and decided he was cooked.

DAMNED RUSSELL VOIGHT. Completely infuriating. Always brewing for a fight with her. At least, that was what it felt like. Still, Elizabeth Brooks was in trouble and had come to Penny hoping to make a deal with the FBI. It was Penny's rotten luck that the lead agent on the Colin Heath case happened to be one she'd previously dismantled in court. Not that it had been his fault. During her research, she'd discovered an exemplary investigator and had prepared for him like no other witness.

Now, from his side of this deal, special agent Russell Voight could create all sorts of chaos for Penny's client.

"I have a client to protect. As you know, *Russell,* Colin Heath is dangerous and Elizabeth has a son to raise."

He gave her the hard stare. He probably didn't like being called Russell. Too bad, because calling men by their given names with just a hint of sarcasm had been a trick Penny used to maximum effect. She called it the Mommy Game and she hadn't met a man yet who could withstand it.

"Which is exactly why I won't let you screw around. We're either making a deal, Penny, or we're not. No games. Are you in or out?"

Huh. Maybe the Mommy Game wasn't so surefire with this particular man.

"Of course I'm in. You need to give me assurances, though. I won't have the feds leaving my client—or her son—to face a murderer."

"What's with the son? That's the second time you've brought him up."

Because I'm terrified for him. Penny sighed. Blame it on the madman who'd opened fire on the courthouse today, but the plan she'd mapped out for this conversation had evaporated, simply imploded under the terror that came with watching those around her, including her father, drop to the ground. Standing on those steps, for a few brief seconds she'd thought her father was dead, shot down in front of her eyes. The panic from earlier whipped inside her, curling her stomach into tight knots, each one of them squeezing, squeezing, squeezing.

She glanced back at Russ, hands on his lean hips, all chiseled face and alpha among alphas, and her stomach let up. She'd guessed his height to be around five-ten, but he carried enough power and presence to fill a giant. With Russ came a sense of strength. Control. She didn't doubt he could be a hothead, but he also understood how to maneuver a conversation.

She let out a breath. "I have to be able to trust you."

"Be straight with me and you can trust me. I've been working this case for over a year. Don't waste my time. Don't waste the bureau's time. If my guess is right, Colin Heath is running this scam in multiple states. We've got agents all over the country chasing leads on this guy."

Penny held her hand to the chair, but he stared down at her, eyes a little squinty. "Please sit. I'll tell you everything I know."

He sat. *Woo-hoo!* At least she'd kept him from leaving. Back to work here. "As you know, Elizabeth Brooks is a licensed stockbroker."

"Correct."

"After the husband's murder, Colin Heath realized there was money unaccounted for."

"You're telling me Sam Brooks was ripping off Heath?"

She nodded.

"Of course he was. What do these animals expect? They rip off innocent people and then expect their partners not to make off with the profits?"

Penny waited a moment. Russ remained silent. Her turn to speak again. "Right. So, Colin went to Elizabeth soon after Sam's death and told her the money was missing. Obviously, he wanted it, but she didn't know anything about it."

"Come on, Penny."

Seemed the FBI agent trusted no one. Probably a good trait in an investigator. "It's the truth. She loved her husband. Maybe she suspected a few of his stock deals were off, but when she questioned him, he schmoozed his way around it. She made the mistake of trusting her husband. Women can't be convicted for that."

That got her the hard look he'd leveled on her five months ago from the witness stand. "They can when they're involved in criminal activity."

Penny rolled her eyes. "Heath is as cynical as you are and thought she was lying about not knowing where the money was. He told her she'd have to work off her husband's debt by doing trades for him. She refused and he sent her a photo of her son with an X over his head."

"He threatened her son."

Russ let out a long breath and his shoulders dipped forward. The man had a soft spot for kids. Good to know.

Suddenly, she wondered if he had children. None of her previous research had indicated such. From what she knew, he was in his early thirties and had never been married. Didn't mean he hadn't had a relationship that resulted in a baby. She could have overlooked certain aspects of his personal life.

"Unless she agreed to do the trades," Penny said, "the photo implied her boy would be in danger. So she did it. What devoted mother wouldn't break the law to protect her child? Let's not forget she's a grieving widow. Until last week, she'd been unable to go through Sam's things. When she finally worked up the nerve, she found multiple safe-deposit-box keys hidden in the attic. Those safe-deposit boxes contained five million dollars in cash."

Russ's eyebrows flew up. "Not bad."

"Assuming it was the stolen money, she cleaned out the boxes and took the money to Heath. She figured the debt would be paid and that would be the end of it."

"How naive is this woman?"

Penny shrugged. "More desperate than naive. Heath took the money, but told her she'd have to continue making trades or else… Fearing she'd be prosecuted if she went to the FBI, she came to me."

"And here we are."

"Yes. She wants out. She can give you account numbers, how the scheme works, everything. She just wants a new life somewhere safe."

Penny sat back and waited. She'd done her job and presented her offer. Now the FBI would have to decide how to handle it.

Again, Russ drummed his fingers, his gaze on her, unyielding, analyzing. Trying to figure her angle. No angle. Just an attorney trying to give her client peace of mind.

Penny leaned forward, touched the arm of his chair. "She's a mom, Russell. Her husband is dead and she's trying to make a life for her son. She knows she broke the law. She wants to make it right. Can you help her?"

Russ glanced down at her hand on the armrest, then brought his gaze back to her face. She wouldn't attempt a guess at his thoughts. Cynics tended to surprise her, so she'd long ago given up trying to figure them out.

"Let me talk to my supervisor," he said. "Elizabeth is willing to give us everything? No screwing around?"

First step complete. *Go, Penny.* "No screwing around. I promise."

Someone rapped on her door and she glanced up to see her brother Zac and his girlfriend standing in the doorway. *They're back.* "Hey, guys. Is Dad okay?"

"He's fine. I figured we'd check on you and take you home."

Zac slid a questioning gaze to Russ, then came back to her. Right. Introductions. "Special Agent Voight, this is my brother Zachary and his girlfriend, Emma. Zac and Emma, meet Russell Voight from the FBI"

Emma made an *oh* face. "Are we interrupting?"

As usual, the sight of Emma, her dark hair pulled back in a way that resembled a cute third-grade teacher, settled Penny's rattled nerves. Which was saying something, because not many people in Penny's world had that kind of influence. Funny in an easy, disarming way, she carried a reserved calm about her. Emma, being the complete opposite in all matters concerning looks, fashion, outspokenness and Penny's general affection for chaos, was special.

And considering she'd started out as Penny's client when she'd thrown herself into proving her wrongfully convicted brother's innocence, Penny liked to brag that she'd found Emma before Zac. Depending on the day, Penny either took credit for bringing them together or accused her brother of being a pig for seducing her then client and now close friend.

"I think we're about done here," Russ said, turning toward Zac and Emma.

Zac adjusted his posture, squeaking out a few more millimeters of height while he took stock of the other male in the room. Fascinated, Penny shifted her gaze to Russ's back and the excellent fit of his jacket. At first glance, the differences between Russ Voight and Zac Hennings weren't hard to miss. Where Zac was tall and broad-shouldered with blond hair, Russ Voight's short dark hair stood out. His height clocked in over a few inches shorter than Zac's and maybe his body was more compact, but the set of his shoulders, that thrown-back I'm-in-charge stance, not to mention his predatory grace, indicated all male, all the time. Something churned low in Penny's belly. Maybe it was lower. Lower than her belly, higher than her thighs. Pure sexual attraction.

Russ shook Zac's hand. "You're the Cook County ASA. Criminal Prosecutions Bureau, right?"

Knows Zac. Interesting. Not nearly as interesting as watching these two size each other up the way idiot males often did in their attempt to establish who'd be the lead gorilla in the room.

"Yeah." Zac said.

"Uh-oh, Zachary. The FBI knows who you are. Maybe they're watching you."

Zac shrugged. "Let 'em watch."

Russ glanced back at her. "You're half-right."

"Excuse me?" she said.

"It's part of the shooting investigation. We're looking at motive as to why someone decided to open fire on innocent civilians. Your brother's job—as well as yours—makes him a possibility."

Emma straightened from leaning on the doorframe and stepped fully into the room. "Come again?"

Without moving from his spot, Zac nodded. "People threaten ASAs all the time."

"Correct," Russ said. "We're looking at everything. Including the case your father is currently working."

"Hang on," Penny said. "You think the shooter was aiming at my *father?*"

"Didn't say that."

"Russell!"

He shifted back, tilted his head and gave her a flat-mouthed look. "Can I answer the question before you start hollering?"

Sufficiently chastised, Penny sat back. "Sorry."

Zac folded his arms and grinned. "This, I'm enjoying."

"No kidding," Emma said.

But Penny had had enough of them. "Knock it off, you two. Go ahead, Russell."

Russ swung his gaze to Zac and Emma, then came back to Penny. "*Anyway,* we're looking at every angle. Everything is a possibility."

"You'll keep us updated?"

"Of course. Until we figure this out, though, don't go having press conferences on the courthouse steps. Lay low and stay safe. Got it?"

And—hello, sexy eyes—the power in that dark-chocolate stare set her body to churning again. Normally, she'd say something snarky about being bossed around, but Russ didn't look in the mood to play. She didn't know him well enough to know what he was in the mood for, but if the shadows under his eyes were any indication, sleep might be at the top of his list.

"I've got it," Penny said. "I'll be careful."

"Thank you. We're all set here, then?"

She nodded. "You'll get back to me about that other matter?"

"As soon as I have something, I'll call you."

"Thanks. And thanks for today, too."

Their eyes connected for a few short seconds, that focused and unmistakable recognition of sexual attraction. If Penny would let it happen, Russell Voight could completely unglue her. Which wouldn't necessarily be a bad thing, because heaven knew it took a lot for a man to work her up. Part of being an aggressive woman meant finding a man willing to do battle when necessary. And even when not necessary. Call her crazy, but Penny hungered for the pull of a heated argument. Most of the men she'd come across didn't understand her need for debate or came off as arrogant and unbending.

Thus, the shrinking pool of male candidates strong enough to survive her continued to be a challenge. One thing about Penny Hennings, good or bad, she knew how to bring a man down.

Russ smiled at her, just a small quirk of his lips that let her know he knew her mind had gone somewhere other than Elizabeth Brooks. *Dirty dog.*

"You are very welcome," he said. "I'll call you."

Penny cleared her throat. Gah. *Quit acting love struck.*

"I'll walk you out," Zac said.

The minute the men left the room, Emma swooped in. "Wow."

Play dumb. Penny motioned Emma to the chair Russ had just vacated and the two of them sat. "Wow, what?"

This earned her a rather obnoxious snort from her dear friend. "Come on. You think I didn't notice you looking at him like he was a giant pile of white gummy bears?"

Penny scrunched her face. "Hey, now, don't say that."

"Why?"

On the list of Penny's all-time favorite candies, white gummy bears claimed the top spot. She didn't just love them; she craved them with a ferocious yearning that kept her up at night, dreaming of the quick shot of sweetness hitting her system. No matter how many times she'd sworn them off, they always lured her back, teased her into submitting. When it came to white gummy bears, she was no better than the crack addicts swarming the South Side of Chicago.

"Because they make me feel weak. I don't want a man making me feel that way."

Emma tilted her head and puckered.

"Please," Penny said. "Now you're psychoanalyzing me? Listen, Freud, it's nothing deep. I'm just saying I don't want to feel needy when it comes to men."

"Yeah, but you said you don't want to be weak. You've never been weak a day in your life."

"Exactly my point."

Emma scoffed. "Maybe that's your problem."

Problem? She didn't have any problems. "And what's *that* supposed to mean?"

"It means I always knew you were a little nuts, but until now, I didn't realize how deep your level of nuttiness ran."

Only Emma could get away with saying that. And worse, rather than being insulted, Penny laughed. What had she ever done without Emma? Truly, it would have been a travesty if this woman hadn't come into her life.

"You're lucky I love you, Emma Sinclair."

"I love you, too, which is why I will risk bodily injury and say this to you. Relationships are about partners. One is vulnerable when the other is strong. Then it switches back. It's about balance. You think your brother doesn't feel vulnerable sometimes? That guy worries about his job like no other. Makes me crazy, but I also love that about him. And trust me, he's far from weak."

Why were they even discussing this? "I see your point. It doesn't matter, though. Russ Voight is off-limits. He's working a case involving a client. And, unlike my pig of a brother, who got involved with you while working your case, I'm not doing it. Uh-uh."

Emma laughed. "You know he's not a pig. You just say that to get him riled."

Penny did a fast clap. "I know. It's such fun."

Zac swung into the room. "What's fun?"

"Nothing," they both said.

He eyeballed them. "You're talking about me again?"

"We are," Penny said.

For what might be the thousandth time since Zac began seeing Emma, he threw his arms up. He didn't like his girlfriend talking to his sister about him. *Too bad, big brother.* "Relax. Is Russ gone?"

"Yeah. He seems like a good guy. Some of those feds are cocky SOBs."

"He's good. I destroyed him on the stand a few months back and he still talks to me. Heck, he saved my life today. Some of the guys I've gone against probably keep a bullet with my name on it."

Her brother poked his finger at her. "Exactly why you need to follow Voight's instructions and lay low."

She didn't want to believe her father had been the target of a shooting. Could someone hate them that much?

American citizens deserved to have their constitutional rights protected and that was her job. Invariably upon meeting someone, she'd be asked what was known by defense attorneys as the "cocktail party question." The old "How can you defend them?" and nothing provoked Penny like that blasted question. For her it was about judgment, and implying that being a defense lawyer was somehow less worthy than being a prosecutor. As if she took joy in defending a man accused of murder. In truth, many nights she lost sleep over it.

Reality was she couldn't resist the job. Call her a masochist but she loved the unwinnable case. Loved the inevitable problems and the intellectual challenge.

The war.

"This may shock you, Zachary, but I will follow his advice. I may be crazy, but I'm not stupid. Still, the idea that Dad was targeted because he defended someone's rights seems hypocritical. Not that I understand the criminal mind."

"Amen to that," Zac said. He rapped his knuckle on the door. "Get packed up. I'm hungry and I'm tired."

"A deadly combination," Emma deadpanned.

Zac threw her the king of hairy eyeballs. *Oh, boy.* Knowing just how crabby her brother could be when his sugar crashed, Penny closed her laptop, unplugged it and shoved it into her messenger bag. "Don't fight. Please. I've had enough conflict for one day. I mean, seriously, it's not every day someone tries to kill me."

Chapter Three

Russ badged his way into Gerald Hennings's office, parked in one of the guest chairs and waited for him to get off the phone. It was 10:00 a.m. and the day had already gone to hell. As of 7:43 a.m., after surviving a surgery that would have killed most, the reporter who'd been shot on the courthouse steps was no longer among the living.

This development had Russ reprioritizing his caseload just when he'd gotten traction on Heath. He wanted to nail that guy and send him away for a good long time.

For years, Russ had been chasing guys like Heath, guys who would rob senior citizens and hardworking people of their life's savings. His own parents had been victimized by a mortgage scammer, and from the day his childhood home had been foreclosed on, Russ let his hurt and anger fuel him on the job. On the days he got sick of the lowlifes, he thought of the morning, at age twelve, he'd stood on the front lawn watching his father turn over the keys to their home. A sight like that didn't leave a man.

Ever.

Hennings set his phone in the cradle and relaxed back in his chair. Fit for a man his age, he was legendary in Chicago for his pristine appearance. Rarely had his expertly cut salt-and-pepper hair been seen out of place. Add to that his custom shirts and flashy suspenders, and reporters all over the city now referred to him as Dapper DL, short for Dapper Defense Lawyer.

"Good morning, Agent Voight."

Russ leaned over the desk and shook his hand. "Morning, sir."

"You have an update for me?"

"I do. I'm not sure if you've heard, but the reporter involved in the shooting died this morning."

"I did hear that. Tragedy. We'll send our condolences." He shook his head. "I'll never understand what drives someone to do this."

Yeah, well, maybe you shouldn't defend these monsters. That was another conversation, though. Right now he had news and, figuring Gerald Hennings liked his bad news brief and to the point, he dived in. "I'm not at liberty to give you details, but we've seen enough evidence to suggest you may have been the target of the shooting yesterday."

To the man's credit, he didn't react. His face remained neutral. No raised eyebrows, no frown, not even a blink. Russ supposed years of defending scumbags had honed his body-language skills.

"I see," he said. "And you're sure it was me? Not Penny?"

That, Russ couldn't say. "We're not a hundred percent. You and Penny were in close proximity to the shooting and reporters generally aren't targeted that often. With the location involved, there is likely a bigger issue as opposed to a random shooting."

Hennings finally gave him some body language and rolled his bottom lip out. "Something tells me that's not the only reason you're here."

Smart man. Russ nodded. "We're arranging protection for you, Penny and Zac."

"You think that's necessary?"

"We'd rather play it safe while we're investigating. You can expect more questioning today, and we're coordinating with the U.S. Marshals to get you protection."

If the man had any issues with the plan, he gave no indication of it. Too bad he was a defense lawyer. He'd make a damned fine FBI agent.

"I appreciate that," Hennings said. "When can we expect someone? I need to tell Zac. And my daughter."

Lucky him. "It'll be today."

"Good." He propped his elbows on the desk, ran both hands over his perfect, albeit thinning, styled hair, then cracked a smile. "Would it be considered bribing an officer if I paid you a hundred dollars to tell Penny?"

And damn if he didn't like this guy. "You're apprehensive about the protection?"

"No. I'm apprehensive about telling my stubborn daughter a marshal will be tagging along wherever she goes. You'd better find someone with stamina. She'll debate everything."

Don't I know it? Then again, an assignment like this, minus the hundred bucks, might be one Russ could cherish. He'd hold this sucker in his heart for the rest of his life.

"Sir, five months ago, your daughter subjected me to the most brutal cross-examination I have ever endured. She whipped me so hard I'm still bleeding."

Hennings's smile went full-blown. Clearly the man adored his daughter. "I taught her well."

"You did. Which I should be ticked at you about, but I'm going to help you out here. You keep your hundred bucks, because after that beating she put me through, I'd love nothing more than to tell her that when it comes to her safety, she'll have to do exactly what I say. That will be the most fun I've had in years."

PENNY HUSTLED ACROSS the flooded Chicago street barely beating the walk signal and almost getting plastered by a cabbie who'd obviously had too much caffeine.

Caffeine overload was exactly her intention on this short trip from her office in the adjacent building. Considering sleep had eluded her most of the night, the double-shot latte might do the trick. Being the freak of nature she was, five hours of slumber each night was all she needed. Mostly. Last night she'd been woefully short. Apparently, being the victim of a crazed sniper wasn't conducive to restful sleep.

Don't think about it. She pushed through the revolving door of Erin's Gourmet Coffee, where the frigid air—a lovely relief from the unseasonably vicious heat—and the aroma of fresh coffee welcomed her. Add Erin's acclaimed hot scones and Penny went into sensory overload. *Come to me, baby.*

She stepped to the back of the four-deep line and glanced around. Not an open table to be had. Just as well. She'd told the receptionist she'd only be a few minutes. No time to dawdle. And since when did she like to dawdle? If this was what a lack of sleep did, she wanted no part of it. Building a great law career meant no breaks when she should be studying case files.

Her cell phone rang and she slipped it from her jacket pocket. Blocked number. This should be good. Being a defense attorney, blocked numbers always proved somewhat entertaining. Could be a paranoid client. Could be a potential client. Could be a whole host of things that would turn her ho-hum day into one heck of a humdinger.

She hit the button before the call went to voice mail, then stuck a finger in her ear to silence the echoing conversations of the packed shop. "Penny Hennings," she said in her tough-as-nails lawyer voice.

"Ah, the lovely Penny Hennings. I'm surprised you took my call."

"Well, you shouldn't be, since your number is blocked and I don't know who this is. If you didn't expect me to pick up, why call?"

"This is Colin Heath."

Penny shoved the phone away and stared at it. Had the thing shifted to animal form? Never before had she received a call from a man one of her clients was about to testify against.

Suddenly, her father's voice boomed in her head, advising her to forget her nerves. To approach her subject in that cool, collected way she'd practiced for years and then, when the moment presented itself, to slowly lure her prey in and strike.

Even if her prey was a murderous madman.

She put the phone back to her ear. "According to you, this is Colin Heath, but theoretically you could be anyone."

"Defense lawyers. Always so suspicious."

Comes with the territory, buddy.

The woman behind her made an effort of clearing her throat. The line had moved, but Penny hadn't. She turned to the woman. "Sorry."

Needing to concentrate, she stepped out of line and walked to an empty corner near the pastry case. "What can I do for you, Mr. Heath?"

"Oh, my love, call me Colin. After all, I let you live yesterday."

A slow burn curled inside her. "What do you mean, you let me live?"

"I've been watching Elizabeth Brooks. She's talking to you. Advise her to forget my name. Her husband stole from me and he knew the risks that posed."

Movement at the door drew her gaze and a dark-haired—and stone-faced—Russ Voight strode in. *What the heck?* He scanned the crowded shop, spotted her and beelined to her.

She threw her hand up before he spoke and pointed at the phone. "Mr. *Heath,* why are you calling me? If you're looking for an attorney, obviously I can't help you."

Russ gawked. At any other time, she'd have laughed that the sexy FBI agent's chiseled features had suddenly gone soft and horrified, but right now she was too freaked to consider it funny.

"Oh, but you can help," Heath said. "Tell Elizabeth to

keep that lovely mouth of hers shut and I will continue to let you live."

What? Penny stood tall. "That's the second time you've said that. Explain."

"On the courthouse steps. That was my shooter, Ms. Hennings. He's quite good. In all that chaos, he managed not to hit you or your dear father. Your options are these. You either stop working with Elizabeth Brooks or get her to keep quiet. If you do that, she and that boy of hers will stay alive. I'd hate to see him grow up without at least one parent."

The slow burning inside Penny erupted to a full-blown volcano. Needing something to do—other than hunt down Colin Heath and strangle him—she latched on to Russ's suit sleeve and twisted. Just a vicious grip that made her knuckles pop. To Russ's credit, he took the assault on his person in stride.

This crazed lunatic thought he'd use her to threaten a client. Not. Ever.

Russ swiveled two fingers between her eyes and his. *Focus,* he mouthed.

She threw her shoulders back, breathed in and let calm, fierce lawyer Penny take hold. As lawyer Penny, no one could beat her. She pictured Colin Heath in the witness box, waiting for her to decimate him—to shred him.

Go.

"Clearly you're aware that you're threatening me. I could have you arrested. And it would be the least of your crimes."

What? Russ mouthed.

Penny held her finger up. *I got this, fella.*

"But you won't," Heath said. "If you did, I'd have you killed. Even from prison I can make it happen. I could do it right now. Or when you leave the coffee shop."

He knew where she was. Searing heat shot to her cheeks. Fear? Maybe. Because there was something incredibly weakening about a murderer stalking her.

Shifting sideways to peer around Russ, she studied each

table. In the corner, two men sat in deep conversation. Couldn't be Heath. The next two tables had been pushed together by a group of moms out for morning coffee with their toddlers. A young guy, maybe twenty, sat at one table, reading a magazine. Too young.

"What?" Russ finally said.

She put her hand over the receiver and got right next to his ear. "He knows I'm in here."

"Don't worry," Heath said. "I'm not in the store with you. I wouldn't be that foolish. Tell the FBI agent I see him, too."

Heaven help her. Where was this man?

She looked up at Russ again, focused on his dark eyes instead of the fear making her tremble. He stuck his bottom lip out—thinking—and rolled his hand.

Keep talking. Easy for him to say. He hadn't just been threatened by a psycho who'd decided opening fire on innocent people would be a good way to prove a point.

A woman squeezed behind Russ to peruse the offerings in the bakery case and he inched forward, shook his head. She understood. A packed coffee shop wasn't exactly a great place to have this conversation, but she wasn't about to step outside and make herself a target. Again.

Trapped in a damned coffee shop and she couldn't even get any caffeine.

Russ glanced into the hallway behind them, where one of the coffee-guzzling moms had just exited the restroom.

He grabbed Penny's wrist, dragged her down the hall, where her enormous heels clicked and clacked against the tile. Finally, she and Russ swung into the bathroom. The barely-big-enough-for-one bathroom left them a few inches apart, and the heady mix of his soap—spice and leather—brought the memory of Russ on top of her the day before, giant erection and all, to mind.

Too close.

She scooted back and bumped the toilet. Ew. Sideways. Only way to go. Russ must have sensed her discomfort, though, and, hero that he was, backed against the door to give her any available space.

"Lovely Penny?"

And how annoying was that whole lovely-Penny nonsense? *Crush him.*

"Let me get this straight," she said to Heath. "You want me to convince my client not to testify against you. In exchange you will leave her and her son alone. Why not just kill them both?"

Heath laughed. Not that she expected him to answer that question. As an attorney she was ethically bound to report any crime she'd been made aware of. Worse, he'd been careful not to give Penny specifics about the threat he'd made against her. Yesterday alone she'd threatened to kill someone five times. Didn't mean she'd do it. Right now, she had nothing worth reporting. Oh, this was a calculating man. He knew exactly where the line was.

"My offer is on the table, lovely Penny."

"You realize if I try to talk her out of testifying she could get another attorney."

"She could, but people might get hurt. With this sudden guilty conscience of hers, she couldn't live with it. But, alas, you won't let that happen. Too many lives at risk. Yours, hers, the boy's. Even your family."

Her *family.* She slapped her hand over her head, stared hard at Russ as a wave of emotion so raw and ravaging tore into her, made her skin burn. What would keep Heath from going after them? Her mother, her father. What about Zac, Mr. Predictable? He stopped at the same coffee shop every morning on his way to work. Every morning. Same time. Same location. One by one, this maniac could pick off her family.

Gently, Russ set his hand on top of hers and squeezed. "Breathe," he whispered. "Relax."

Closing her eyes, she focused on next steps. On getting this psycho locked up. Yes. That was what she'd do.

"I understand," she said into the phone.

"How many lives will be lost, Penny? It's up to you. I'll phone you in twenty-four hours. Give me the right answer."

The line went dead and Penny sucked in a massive breath, and the tight walls pressed in and the shiny white tiles swayed and danced. The phone slipped from her fingers, clattered to the floor. She'd have to sterilize the thing. Or throw it out. Russ bent low, scooped it up, and she scrunched her nose. The germs alone… He hit the button, obviously to be sure the call ended.

He shoved the phone into his jacket pocket and grasped her arm. "You all right?"

"I may throw up."

"You're in the right place."

She nodded because, well, he had a point there. Only, she didn't want to be on her knees in this bathroom. Who knew the last time the floor was washed?

The pattern on the wall behind Russ looped and swirled and Penny swayed. Massive head rush.

Grasping her arms, he held her steady. "Uh-oh."

She leaned forward, rested her head against his shoulder. She needed a minute. Not even. Just a few seconds to let the dizziness pass and consider facing such a catastrophic situation.

Russ ran his hands up and down her arms, a gentle re-assurance that allowed her to close her eyes—only for a minute—and get herself together.

Finally, she backed away, met Russ's gaze. "You know he's insane."

"I DO KNOW THAT." He squeezed her arms. "If I let go, you're not going to face-plant, are you?"

Penny scoffed. "On this floor? Not on your life."

A few minutes ago, her skin had turned that ashy-gray that preceded going lights out, and he'd take no chances on her smacking her head against the john and getting a concussion.

Slowly, he lifted his hands from her arms and held them out.

Only slightly annoyed at her own weakness, Penny waved him off. "He ordered that shooting yesterday. To scare me."

"He said that?"

She nodded.

He snatched his phone from his pocket and scrolled through his contacts. When he'd entered the shop, he'd had every intention of tearing into Penny for walking across the street alone. He'd told her the night before they were looking into the idea of either her or her father being targets and clearly she'd blown that off. She was damned lucky the receptionist squealed on her whereabouts or she'd be dealing with this Heath garbage on her own. In the middle of a crowded coffee shop, no less!

Crazy woman.

"Who are you calling?"

"My office. I want marshals on you ASAP. We'll get Elizabeth protection also. How the hell did he find out she wants a deal? And why the hell are you walking around alone when you almost got shot yesterday?"

Penny's face stretched into an appalled openmouthed gape. "You have lost your mind, *Russell.* I'll go wherever I want. And I have no idea how Heath knows about Elizabeth. Aside from my coworkers, you're the only one I spoke to about it. And I'm sure Elizabeth hasn't told anyone. At least, no one outside her immediate family. And she's so nervous, I'm not sure she'd have done even that. He said he's watching her, though. Maybe he took a shot and got lucky."

"Yeah, well, that lucky shot just earned him extortion and obstruction charges to go with his landslide of financial-fraud issues. And if I can prove it, murder. The reporter died this morning." Penny reeled back and he held up a finger when Guy Hawkins, one of his squad mates on the CID—Criminal Investigation Division—answered. "Voight here. Where are we on those marshals for Penny and Gerald Hennings?"

"They're on their way over. Should be there anytime."

At his hip, the door lever moved. Someone trying to use the john. "One second," he said to the person on the other side. He went back to Hawkins. "Good. Thanks. Put me through to Everly." Russ looked back at Penny, who stared at him with dead eyes. The reporter thing rattled her. Rightly so. "Trying to reach my ASAC. Voice mail."

Not a break to be had. He left a message. Only thing to do.

"Okay," he said. "We've got to get out of this bathroom. I'm not taking you out the front door. Who the hell knows where Heath is, but he had a view of the entrance. We know that."

"And what? We're going out the back?"

"I'll have one of the marshals pick us up in the alley. Wherever Heath is, he won't see you leave."

"Where are we going?"

"To find Elizabeth. We'll stash her away somewhere. This guy is soiling himself over whatever she knows. And if he orchestrated that shooting, she knows enough to put him away."

The person in the hallway knocked. "Only one bathroom, chief," a man said.

Russ turned, yanked open the door and flipped his badge up. The young guy, the one he'd spotted reading a *Sports Illustrated* when he'd walked in, stared at the giant letters that read *F-B-I* and his eyes widened. "Oh, wow."

"Yeah," Russ said. "Give us a second."

The kid nodded and Russ shut the door again. Sometimes his love of flashing his badge was borderline perverse.

"I totally need an FBI badge," Penny cracked.

"It's handy. You ready?"

She nodded and Russ opened the door. *Sports Illustrated* guy looked at Penny, then to Russ and back to Penny again. His mouth curved into a sarcastic grin that Russ would have liked to pound away at, but hell, two people spending extended time in a single bathroom conjured all sorts of thoughts. Nothing he could do about that.

Penny stepped into the hallway and jerked her head at the young guy. "All yours. *Chief.*"

Nice. Why he was surprised at her sarcasm, he'd never know. Despite being followed, threatened and shot at, Penny Hennings still had fight in her.

If he could get over the fact that she put criminals back on the street, she might be the love of his life.

Penny stopped in the hallway and turned to him. She bit her top lip, then blew out a breath, and that was so not good.

Ushering her out of the path, he leaned one shoulder against the wall. "You're thinking. What about?"

"My family. He could go after them." Her voice squeaked like the last neglected wheel.

No, no, no. She was not turning tail on him. Not Killer Cupcake, who never shied away from conflict. At least, not that he knew of. He'd worked too long and hard to nail this guy. Between the fraud charges and conspiracy to commit murder, this guy was toast. All they had to do was prove it. The widow's testimony would help them win this. And he wasn't about to let Penny—the defense attorney—wreck it.

"You're not backing down on me, Penny. This case is too important. We'll get all of you protection."

Her mouth dropped open. "You think I'm backing down? *That's* what you think? I happen to be tired. Doesn't mean I'm letting that nutcase dictate how I should live, but I need my family safe. *That's* what I'm thinking."

Could be he blew that call. Could be? With the cremating stare she gave him? Yeah, he'd definitely blown it.

Sports Illustrated guy came out of the john, spotted them and averted his gaze. At least he'd learned his lesson about the beautiful blonde and her sharp tongue. He didn't want any piece of her now.

Neither did Russ. By his estimation, he needed damage control here. He nodded toward the guy. "I think you scared the hell out of him."

Penny rolled her eyes and boosted off the wall. "Don't even try it, Russell. Admit you screwed up. Feeding my ego won't replace that."

Sick bastard that he was, this could definitely be love. "I screwed up. Shouldn't have assumed. And you know what else?"

A noise from the café drew her attention for a second and her ponytail flew over her shoulder when she came back to him. "What?"

Gently, he swept the blond strands over her shoulder, let the backs of his fingers linger a second. Maybe two.

She shifted and he smiled at the punch of physical attraction. Or maybe he needed sex. Hot, sweaty, knock-him-sideways sex that he hadn't had in way too long. Getting busy with a woman had never been a problem. Getting busy with the right woman proved to be a challenge.

Penny Hennings—defense lawyer or not—might be the right woman.

She shifted again, made snoring noises, and he ducked his head closer. Slowly, she lifted her chin, and if he pushed it, if he nudged a little farther, he'd be close enough to kiss her. "Yeah, you might be the right one."

Drifting closer, she blinked up at him, those big blue eyes questioning. "I'm sorry?"

A shrill beeping filled the hallway. Phone. The boss returning his SOS call. He shook his head and let the annoying beep get him back in line before he did something beyond stupid.

Sex with Penny Hennings. He'd never survive.

Chapter Four

Once in the unmarked car driven by Brent Thompson, her newly assigned U.S. marshal, Penny and Russ were driven to an FBI safe house near New Buffalo, Michigan, for crying out loud. *Hey, boys, I have nothing whatsoever going on today—let's drive to Michigan.* Anything happening at her office would have to wait. It wouldn't make her clients happy, but her choices were limited.

They'd spent over an hour looping around the lake, and now, as they drove along this quiet road, miles and miles of sparkling Lake Michigan water laid a perfect path against a bright blue sky. It seemed all that water led straight to Heaven. She didn't visit the beach often, but driving along this road, watching sunbathers and toddlers playing in the sand, the sunlight shimmering off the lake, all of it gave her a sense of calm she didn't often feel. Maybe she should make more of an attempt to spend time at her parents' lake house in Wisconsin.

"You're too quiet back there," Russ said from the front passenger seat. "That scares me."

"Poor baby. Relax, Russell. I was thinking about going to the beach."

"I didn't peg you as a beach person."

"I'm not. Might be time for that to change. Are we almost there?"

According to Russ, Elizabeth Brooks and her son would

be meeting them at the safe house, where they'd stay under guard of the U.S. Marshals. At least she'd be safe while Penny tried to figure a way out of this mess.

She reached into her bag for her phone, then remembered Russ had taken it from her. Maddening, this man. He didn't trust her to not make calls and literally confiscated the phone. Then he promptly removed the battery to ensure the phone couldn't be tracked. Colin Heath had gone to great lengths to get her attention. After the brazen shooting on the courthouse steps, his being able to bribe someone at the phone company for her location didn't seem like a stretch.

Penny sighed and Russ spun to her. "Problem?"

"I stink at being idle. All this doing nothing makes me twitchy."

"We're almost there. You need to call someone? You can use my phone."

She'd already checked in with her dad before they left the city. Last he'd seen her, she'd walked across the street for a latte, one she never did get and still desperately needed. Her dad had promised to either move or cover her client meetings for the day, but still, she felt like a slacker.

"No. Thank you. You have people watching my family, right?"

He nodded. "I'm on it. Trust me on this, okay? You all have protection. If we find your family needs to be in a safe house, we'll deal with it."

Penny swung her gaze to the back of Marshal Thompson's—Brent's—head. Smart man that he was, he kept his eyes on the road, pretending he couldn't hear any of this conversation. "If I didn't trust you, I wouldn't be sitting here."

With that, Russ turned front again and didn't speak for another twenty minutes until they pulled into the driveway of a white beach cottage with large, covered windows. The house didn't look all that big, but she knew from her parents' lake home there might be a ton of property behind it where the house cascaded onto the beachfront. Heck of a safe house. This baby had to have been seized during an investigation. She'd grill Russ about it later.

A curving brick walkway led to the porch, but Russ jumped out, punched in the garage-door code on the keypad and Brent pulled in.

This would be Elizabeth's new home until the FBI figured out how to save her life. Or maybe Penny would figure it out first. Either way, Colin Heath would be brought down.

Brent killed the engine, and Penny, needing freedom, yanked on the handle. The door didn't move. Seriously? They'd locked her in. As if *she* was the criminal.

"You boys think I'm going somewhere?"

"Nope. Waiting on Russ to close the garage door so no one sees you. Smart-mouth."

Penny hooted and—wow—it felt so good to laugh. Even if Brent had struck her as a little pushy and overbearing with the way he'd ordered her into the car at the coffee shop. She preferred verbally sparring with someone who didn't confuse her—the way Russ did. She didn't know what she wanted from Russ. She liked bickering with him, but sometimes she wanted something else. Something quiet and calm and…and…protective. She squeezed her eyes shut. Protection from a man. When did that stop being the plague?

"Nothing to say?" Brent cracked.

"Oh, I have plenty to say. And you and I will get along just fine."

Finally, Russ opened her door and she nearly knocked him over leaping out.

"Head inside and stay there while we check the perimeter. We had agents clear the inside already, but I want another look outside."

Penny snapped to attention and saluted. "Sir, yes, sir. Why don't I just wait here until you do your thing? Make it easier on all of us."

He held a finger up. "Even better. Don't move."

Sure. Fine. What she needed was a barrel of gummy bears. Sugar right now would be excellent.

The two men walked to the back of the garage to the solid wood door—no windows to be broken by would-be intruders.

Ten minutes later, in the suffocating heat of the closed garage, the back door opened and Brent stepped through. He whirled his finger at her. "We're good. Perimeter is clear."

"Where's Russ?"

A loud sucking noise came from the opposite corner of the garage and she spun backward. *What's that?* Russ stood in the doorway kicking at the weather stripping—*terrorized by weather stripping?*—on the bottom of the door leading to the house. She slapped her hand over her chest.

"Scared the hell out of me, *Russell!*"

He snapped his head up and jiggled keys at her. "I went in the back door. We're all set in here."

Penny marched up the three wooden steps and swung by Russ into a mudroom the size of a small office. "How far out is Elizabeth?"

"Twenty minutes."

Russ waved her through the second door into the sunny yellow kitchen and its cozy breakfast nook. Cute, but the real deal was straight ahead, where hand-carved walnut floors led to an open living room and floor-to-ceiling windows overlooked the lake. Penny wandered the room, running her fingers over stuffed pillows and shelves holding clay pitchers and bowls. She imagined snuggling up on the huge sofa. And if a sexy FBI agent wanted to join her, that wouldn't be a problem.

Gummy bears. *Think about the gummy bears.*

She glanced back at said agent. "This place looks like a Pottery Barn catalog. You feds know how to treat a witness."

"We seized it last year. Stockbroker turned Ponzi schemer."

She'd hit that one right. Russ flipped a switch on the wall

and sent the drapes sliding closed. *No.* The man was killing her fantasy of the two of them curled up, watching the afternoon sun skitter across the lake.

"Can we leave those open? The view is amazing."

"If we can see out, people can see in. They shouldn't have been open in the first place."

Point there. So much for fantasies. Penny sighed.

"Now my life is complete," Russ said.

"How's that?"

"You being…wistful."

"Wistful?"

Please.

But he stared right at her, those dark eyes devouring hers. So-oh-oh sexy.

"I liked it. The softer side of Penny Hennings. Another facet to a fascinating package."

As if she believed that. "*You* think I'm fascinating? The FBI agent who hates defense attorneys."

He propped a hip on the arm of the sofa and crossed his arms. Casual, but guarded. "I don't hate defense attorneys."

"You said—"

"I hate that defense attorneys get criminals off. I don't hate you. In truth, I rather enjoy you."

Hello, fantasy. If he kept this up, she'd have those curtains open in the next ninety seconds. There they'd be, the most unlikely pair the justice system ever saw, sprawled across that sofa, doing things she hadn't done in a very—very—long time.

"Russell—"

The hum of a motor—garage door going up—sounded and Russ turned. *Don't kill this moment.* Except Brent appeared, his hulking body filling the kitchen doorway.

"Elizabeth Brooks and her son are here. Kid's going nuts over the lake." He glanced at Penny. "Kids are tough. Always wandering. I'm going to check the upstairs again before they come in."

Brent disappeared upstairs and Russ waved Penny to the couch. "Have a seat. Want something?"

Oh, she wanted something. For a brief second, the room went silent, not a breath to be heard while Russ stared at her and she stared back, the two of them charging the current streaming in the room. Her stomach clenched. Maybe other things clenched, too. At this point, Brent and the entourage that had just pulled up were about to get booted for ten minutes.

Whew. *Hot in here.*

"Penny?"

"Caffeine. Anything with caffeine. And some white gummy bears. I love gummy bears."

Not that her system needed any more activity, but she still mourned the latte she never got at Erin's.

"Gummy bears will have to wait. I'll see what else we've got."

Russ came back with two cans of cola—one diet, one regular. Smart man to not assume she'd want the diet.

She took the diet. It wasn't a double-shot latte, but it would do. Another marshal—this one not as big—came through the mudroom, followed by Elizabeth and her son, Sam. The boy's eyes were big and round and dark like his father's had been—at least from the pictures Penny had seen. In those eyes there was sadness no twelve-year old should know.

And just seconds ago, Penny had been entertaining wicked thoughts about Russ. How awful could she be? She had clients to care for and she was acting like a high-school twit.

She leaped off the couch, went to Elizabeth and, setting the lawyer persona aside for a second, hugged her. They'd given the woman a rushed explanation and thirty minutes to pack. She probably needed a friend as well as an attorney right now. "I'm sorry for the short notice."

"It's okay. If it came from you, I knew it was necessary."

Penny backed away, spotted Brent on the stairs. He gave a thumbs-up. She set a hand on Sam's shoulder. "Hey, pal. My guess is there are a few bedrooms up those stairs. How about you and your mom go up and pick a room?"

"Really?"

"Yep. You're going to have a little vacation here."

One in which you will barely be allowed outside. She wouldn't say that, though. Certain things were better left unsaid.

Penny turned to Brent. "They can go up, right?"

"All clear. We'll be outside. Everyone stays inside. Holler if you need anything."

Elizabeth and Sam made their way upstairs, their footsteps clunking on the wood and echoing through the ceiling.

Russ flopped onto the sofa and stretched his arms across the back. "What do you need?"

She needed a lot of things. Things she wanted him to give her. She cocked her head, then took the chair across from him. No chance she'd risk being on the same sofa. Not with the heat they'd conjured a few minutes ago. That kind of heat had no place in this house when there was a woman and her son who needed their lawyer to be focused. No, sirree.

"You're thinking," he said. "I can see it. You do this thing with your eyebrows. They sort of come up and together. It's your tell."

"Really? Huh."

"I saw it in court that day. Right before you fried my intestines."

"Russell, get over it already."

He smiled, all sweet-talking, good-looking boy, and her stomach hitched again. He did that to her. Made her feel things she shouldn't feel about a man who only wanted to clear a case. *Focus on your client.*

"I like reminding you," he said. "It gets you stirred up and you're fun when you're stirred up."

Men. Pigs. Every one of them. "Heath will call me

tomorrow. I have to tell him something. I'm not sure what that is. So, to answer your question, what I need is to come up with a plan."

"You want my opinion?"

Here's a first. Defense attorney Penny asking an FBI agent—any law-enforcement officer, for that matter—for his opinion. Most law-enforcement members would happily offer an opinion, but it might be more along the lines of Penny taking a trip to hell. She supposed she couldn't blame them, but she knew how to do her job. A job that protected the constitutional rights of American citizens.

Penny leaned her head against the chair cushion. "I'm thinking I should tell him I'll do it. I'll lie to him. Tell him I'll need time to slowly warm Elizabeth up to the idea of not testifying so it looks legit. He can't argue that. He knows she's smart and will be suspicious if I've suddenly changed my mind about her testifying."

"When he calls tomorrow, tell him you'll convince her not to testify. It'll buy us time to question her. Meantime, we're looking for Heath and his shooter from yesterday. We'll talk to people, shake up his contacts. When we find him, we'll lock him up."

Penny pushed her palms into her forehead. "This is insanity. I have to tell my family. We're all in danger."

Russ rose from the sofa and edged around the coffee table, testing his weight on it before sitting down.

A vision of the table collapsing under him flashed and she clucked her tongue. "I'd have loved to have seen you fall flat on your bum if that table collapsed."

He glanced at the table and wiggled on it before grinning at her. "It stinks that you're a defense attorney."

Oh, that playful smile of his might undo her altogether.

"I'll help you with your family," he said. "I'm close to getting this guy and now he's admitted he set up that shooting yesterday. He's desperate. Otherwise, he doesn't make that call." He touched her arm. "It may not seem like it, but you've got the power here. You can destroy this guy."

She barely knew Russell Voight and he'd managed to figure out what she needed. She didn't need to be coddled or patronized or babied. What she needed was to be reminded of her strength. Most men would rush in and tell her what to do. Russ? He told her she had power.

Then he touched her arm and the gentle press blazed inside her. She looked up at him, into those dark eyes that were at once so expressive and yet so distant and she wanted to jump him.

Fast.

Right in this Pottery Barn house with Elizabeth and Sam upstairs and two U.S. marshals outside.

What the hell is wrong with me?

"You okay?" he asked.

No. Wow, she was in deep doo-doo here. She lowered her voice and leaned closer. "I'm totally thinking X-rated thoughts about you."

OF ALL THE WOMEN Russ shouldn't want, Penny Hennings charged him up like no one he'd ever experienced. She drove him out of his mind with the snarky comments and her general distrust of law enforcement. And he still wanted her. Seriously twisted. "How X-rated?" he whispered.

"Russell!"

"Is it triple X or just single?"

Penny slapped her palm against her forehead. "I wasn't thinking *that* detailed. It was a few seconds. That's all. Don't get ahead of yourself."

"Hey, these things are good to know."

She shook her head. "But I shouldn't be thinking that way. We've got a lot going on here and the distraction won't do anyone any good."

"Can I fill you in on something?"

"Sure."

"It's probably a reaction to your string of incidents over two days. I'm the lucky guy here when it happened."

"Says the man who had an erection yesterday?"

He closed his eyes. She had to bring that up.

Finally, he opened his eyes, kept his gaze focused and steady. "Part of it was adrenaline, but part of it wasn't. The part that wasn't is the problem. I'm close to bringing this guy down and your client can make that happen." He ran a finger down her cheek and over her jaw. Something he'd wanted to do every day since he'd first seen her from the witness box.

"Russell—"

"Shh. From the day you shredded me on the stand, I've thought about you. You're beautiful and sexy and mouthy and—freak that I am—that's a huge turn-on. Except the risk is too high."

But, yeah, he wanted to roll in sheets with her. Naked and sweating and exploring.

His presence in her life revolved around Elizabeth Brooks and Colin Heath. Getting emotional about a case created no issues, but he wanted it to be the right emotions. The ones where he went to the wall to lock up the bad guy. Penny in his bed wouldn't make that happen.

Sam's voice sounded from the upstairs hallway and Russ boosted off the table. "We shouldn't talk about this now."

Penny glanced at the staircase, then tapped three fingers against her forehead. "You're right. I'll check on Elizabeth and Sam and we'll get started."

It took twenty minutes for Russ to bring Elizabeth Brooks up to speed. It was all fairly simple. Penny would take the Colin Heath heat while Elizabeth and her son stayed in the safe house, under the protection of U.S. marshals. During that time, she would share with the FBI everything she knew about Heath's pump-and-dump scheme.

Penny, sitting next to Elizabeth on the sofa, touched her

hand. "Are you okay with this? If not, we'll figure something else out."

Uh, no. They wouldn't.

If Russ had to go to war with Penny, no matter how physically attracted to her he was, he'd do it and it would be bloody. He'd busted his tail getting his superiors to sign off on this operation, one that would cost the U.S. taxpayers a nice chunk of change, and he wasn't about to let the lawyer blow his case for him.

"There's nothing else to figure out," he said.

Slowly, Penny angled her head toward him, her nostrils flaring only enough that, had he not studied her body language since the day he'd met her, he would have missed it. That look? The Killer Cupcake look.

"I need a minute with my client," Killer Cupcake said.

Elizabeth shook her head. "That's not necessary. I'll do it. Whatever I need to do to get us out of this, I'll do it."

"She gets immunity," Penny said. "I don't care how the FBI thinks they can implicate her. She gets a pass."

"My superiors have signed off on that. The paperwork is being drawn up."

"You're not questioning my client until everything is signed."

Now I'm done. If she wanted to pull this defense-lawyer bull on him every time, they'd be here awhile. He stood, jerked his head toward the kitchen. "A minute, *counselor.* Please."

"Of course," she chirped.

Damned irritating woman. Even if he did goad her with that *counselor* comment. She stormed into the kitchen, hot on his heels in those stilt shoes, ready for war. Damn, he liked her.

Once in the kitchen, he spun, waved her in and closed the ancient swinging door. One day he'd have a lake house like this. With a goofy swinging door.

He folded his arms and stared down at her mutinous face,

and her blue eyes sparked. He shouldn't have been excited by it. Sickness. Had to be. Because every damned time he saw that look, he wanted to grab her, plant a lip-lock and see how long it took to cool her fire.

Propping her hands on her skirt-clad hips, she huffed, "Well? What is it?"

"We made a deal. You need to trust me."

"First, it's not you I don't trust. It's the FBI. My job is to protect my client's rights. Part of that means having an iron-clad deal before I allow the FBI access to her. What do you not understand about that?"

Was he an idiot now? Some schmuck she could emasculate because she had Ivy League brains and the supermodel looks? *Not happening, babe.* "I know your job. I also know defense lawyers like to annihilate cases guys like me bust their humps on. I'm telling you, you won't derail this."

Instead of the heat and temper he expected to find, her gaze was questioning. Unsure. "Why do you think I'd derail this? I want my client safe. I'm in danger. Getting Heath incarcerated will help all of us."

Damned good point.

One that shut him up. Maybe he was too close to it. Too close to remembering that day when the bank foreclosed on his parents' home because a guy like Heath ran a mortgage scam. Mix that emotional garbage in with his lust for the hot defense lawyer and he had a situation.

He wrapped his fingers around his temples and squeezed in and out, letting the pressure build then release. "Look, we made a deal. In your office. Last night. You can waste time by not letting me question your client or we can get on with it. It's up to you."

She hesitated. Studied the cabinet behind his head, then brought her gaze back to him. Why that response—or lack of one—shocked him, he'd never know. But somewhere deep inside, in a place he didn't like to acknowledge, a place where guys like him shoved all the waste they didn't want to deal with, he absorbed the stab of hurt. "Unbelievable."

She grabbed his forearm. "I trust you. I do. But we both have to be careful here."

"Right," he said. "We'll wait."

"No. That'll be a waste of everyone's time. I have a compromise. Let me talk to my dad. If he's in agreement with going forward, I'll let you question Elizabeth."

She wouldn't make him drive back to the city. A compromise indeed. "You're okay with that? I won't hear any moaning about it?"

"My father is a much better attorney than I am. If he signs off, it's good."

Russ pulled his phone from his pocket. He still had Penny's, minus the battery. "You can't use your phone. Here's mine. I'll give you privacy. Take your time."

She nodded. "Thank you. I think this works for both of us."

"I agree."

He turned to go, not sure how he felt about this compromising Penny. He'd just discovered another hidden facet. The one that saw a solution even if it didn't sync with her original plan. He was hanging on here, clinging to the rail, scrambling for footing so he didn't get sucked into the emotional hell that would be falling for Penny Hennings. The defense lawyer.

"Hey, what you said about your dad being a better lawyer. I don't believe that. He has more experience. Doesn't make him better."

Something happened. Russ wasn't sure what, but Penny flinched. Not just a little, either. "What?" he asked.

"I…I…" She held up her finger. Hesitated. "After the beating I gave you on the witness stand, you should hate me. Instead, you tell me I'm just as good a lawyer as my father."

"It's the truth."

Except, her eyes got a little…misty. *Oh, hell no.* "Penny?"

He took one step—one—and she paddled her hands. "Don't touch me. That'll do me in."

Hello, Confusion, thanks for visiting. "Okay. Sure. Sort of lost here, though."

"You don't get it. From the time I'd been a lowly prelaw student, interning at various firms, doing any grunt work I could find, I've been trying to separate myself from my father's reputation. All to prove I could make it on my own steam. That *nepotism*—" she spat the word, like acid burning her tongue "—hadn't gotten me my spot at one of the top firms in Chicago. It makes me realize all these years of sleepless nights, of studying cases until my mind couldn't absorb any more, was worth it."

"That's good, right?"

"No! You're the man who should hate me and want nothing to do with me. Instead you're the one who gets me."

Who'd have thunk Killer Cupcake had her own spot, deep inside, where she hid all that self-doubt?

She stared at the phone he handed her, ran her thumb over the keypad he'd touched probably thousands of times. "You terrify me. You hate what I do for a living. A job I love. If I survive this Heath mess, it'll most likely be because of your efforts. And that's the rub, because you'll break my heart. I know you will. One way or another, I'll walk away fractured."

Russ opened his mouth. Nothing. Nada. Not one coherent thought. Killer Cupcake had just ripped herself open in front of him and…and…what?

Nothing.

"I'm—"

Her hand shot up. "Let's forget this. Please. Just wipe the last few seconds clean. I'll call my dad, you won't say anything and we will never speak of this again."

She spun away, headed for the mudroom. *Stop her.* He beat her to the door, smacked his hand on it. "What if I want to speak of it again?"

Slowly, she shook her head.

"Not now," Russ said. "After we get through this. When we don't have your client sitting between us. Can we do that?"

He waited a few seconds, stood there like a dummy because Killer Cupcake trusted him enough to evacuate her feelings and it paralyzed him. She'd probably never open up to him again. Maybe that was good, though. Women liked all this emotional upheaval. Men? *Not.* But the idea of Penny shoving all her angst away didn't comfort him much, either. What a mess.

Finally, she tipped her head down, gave a little nod.

Home run. "Okay. Later, then."

She looked up at the door. "I need to pass so I can call my office."

He lifted his hand and opened the door for her. "I'll give you privacy."

Fifteen minutes later, she came through the door again, spotted him leaning against the counter, stopped a few feet from him and held out his phone. "We're good to go."

Chapter Five

"You don't have to walk me in," Penny said to Russ while they waited for the elevator to scoop them up at the garage level of her condo building.

For the nine months Penny had lived in this building, she'd been a believer that the extra monthly fee—convenience tax, as she called it—for a building with a gated garage was worth it. Now, with Colin Heath threatening her, she was sure of it and would never again complain about shoes she could have bought with the convenience-tax money. Even if the slow gate drove her mad, she remained thankful for its presence.

"This is a nice perk," Russ said.

Casual conversation. That was what this was, because she knew that he knew that she knew they were both thinking the universe had royally flipped them off. After the crazy emotional day, one that included the two of them admitting their mutual attraction, the god of love decided this would be the night a judge received a death threat and the extra marshal assigned to Elizabeth Brooks would go to the judge.

Not wanting to leave Elizabeth with only one marshal, Russ and Brent decided Brent would stay behind while Russ drove Penny home. In the morning, Russ would return with Brent's car.

All around a good plan because Elizabeth would be safe. However, Penny was about to step into the elevator leading to her condo—her very empty condo—with the FBI agent her girly parts wanted a piece of. Elizabeth was safe. Penny was not.

She rocked back and forth while the floors blinked off. The doors finally slid open and Russ held them so she could step on. A gentleman to boot. Could this get any worse?

"This is weird," she said.

"Yep."

It wasn't just her overthinking it. That was a relief at least. Still, that throb in her stomach wouldn't quit. The entire ride home she'd felt the pressure, the expanding ball of nerves growing and growing and growing.

"Hey," she said. "We're professionals. We can handle this. What's a little lust?" She nodded toward the elevator buttons. "Eighth floor, big guy."

Russ laughed. "You really are insane."

That would be one way to put it. "It's true. Ask anyone."

When the doors slid open again, Russ stuck his arm out to block Penny's path, then checked the hallway. "All clear. Got your keys?"

"I do."

"Let's go."

She stopped in the hallway outside the elevator and watched the doors close. He needed to be on that elevator. Away from her very empty apartment. Where she wanted to introduce him to an extremely inviting bed.

That throbbing mass in her stomach exploded. Big trouble. "You can go now."

"Sorry, babe. Have to check the apartment."

"Russell!"

"You're the one who said we're professionals. Standard procedure. If Brent were here, he'd do it. Last thing I need is not to do it and have you kidnapped. Although, you're such a pain, they'd probably throw you back."

He laughed at his own joke and Penny gasped, but really, there was a certain amount of pride she could take in scaring off would-be kidnappers. "Russell, I've said it before, flattery will get you everywhere."

Particularly when it comes to my bed.

"I'll keep that in mind."

She spun, marched down the curving corridor and lamented the fact that the plush carpeting absorbed her footsteps. Sometimes a girl wanted to hear her own stomping and this carpet was stealing her fun.

What am I doing? Making herself crazy. That was what. She shook her head to clear the madness, lightened her footsteps and breathed in. Professionals. They could handle it. She'd just let him do his little search while she locked herself in the closet, where she couldn't watch him entering her bedroom. Simple plan.

She focused on her apartment door just ahead. At this hour, most of her neighbors had gone quiet. Mr. Hanley's television was still on, but that was normal, since he was an insomniac. She unlocked the door, pushed it open and waved Russ in. Thank goodness she'd left the place neat.

He glanced around the living room. "You always leave the lights on?"

"Timer. I don't like coming home to darkness."

He nodded in that way that said he really didn't have an opinion on that fact, but didn't necessarily think it odd.

"You mind if I check the rooms?"

"Have at it. I'll know if you go through my underwear drawer."

His only answer was a grunt.

"I guess you could save that for next time, though."

"I'm ignoring you," he yelled from the bathroom.

Penny laughed, and after the long day, laughing felt like that barrel of gummy bears she needed. She stood in the middle of her living room, pondered the closet door while he checked the two bedrooms. Maybe she wouldn't actually get *in* the closet. If she just stared at it, it might be enough to keep her from seeing Russ in her bedroom.

"See anything of interest?" she called.

"Other than the bra you left on your bed?"

Oh, just hell. In a rush that morning, she'd taken the lacy bright pink bra off because—well—she didn't know why. It just hadn't felt right, so she'd swapped it out for a plain beige one and obviously had forgotten to put the sex-kitten one back in the drawer. Once again, the god of love had flipped her off. How could Penny have known Russell Voight would be escorting her home?

"I didn't think I'd have company. In my bedroom."

He stepped into the hallway. "Yeah, well, what's another round of torture?"

Walking toward her, he stopped at the kitchen, smacked on the light, checked the miniscule pantry that a four-year-old wouldn't fit in and turned the light off again.

Then he was in front of her, his tie loose and the button on his collar undone, and if he looked tired, she couldn't blame him. Even she, who functioned on very little sleep, needed her bed.

"I've got a marshal on his way here. He'll stay outside your door tonight."

"Thank you."

For a second, she'd thought about arguing. Pretending to argue, really, because as much as she hated to give in to the fear and weakness of being Heath's prey, the only way she'd sleep was if she knew someone would be there.

Except, this guy Heath, he was a slippery creep and she'd been around slippery creeps long enough to know how they operated.

"Russell, how well do you know these marshals?"

He eyed her. "Why?"

"Heath is insane, but he's also brilliant. He seems to know my every move."

"You think there's a leak somewhere?"

"No. I don't think that. I'm just..." She raised her hands, let them drop. "I don't know. I'm tired."

"Look, it's a valid question. One I've thought of myself. I'm on it. Anyone involved in this case, we're checking their financial records. If Heath has someone on his payroll, we'll find them."

She nodded. "It's probably nothing."

"Doesn't hurt to look. I'm heading to the safe house in the morning. Assuming you want to be there?"

"Yes. I need to go to the office first."

Russ scratched his stubbled chin. "That works. We want everything to look business-as-usual. I'll pick you up at your office and then we'll do some creative driving in case Heath is watching. That work?"

"Sure."

She rocked on her toes again. Here they were, two professionals, having a chat. No problem. Except the snapping energy in the silent apartment made heat fly off Russ in a constant and brutal wave. That wave would suck her under if she wasn't careful.

She pointed to the door. "You should go."

"I know."

"Yet, he stands here. Unmoving."

"Oh, I'm moved. Believe me."

"Russell!"

And still he didn't budge. The only sound was the distant hum from the refrigerator, and Penny concentrated on it rather than that damned loosened tie just begging to be stripped off. And then, the wave swooped in and, as if timed, they both stepped forward and Penny reached for his tie and tugged him to her. His hand slid around the back of her head and she went up on tiptoes, anticipating that first press of his lips. That first moment of their first kiss.

It was more than she'd imagined. He tasted warm and male and so, so, so safe. And then he increased the pressure and she tugged on his tie again, wanting more. So. Much. More.

"Oh, man," he said, his mouth still on hers. "Better than I thought."

"I know. It sucks."

He made a move to pull back, but she gripped his tie, gave it a yank. *You're not going anywhere.* To hell with it. She'd had a miserable couple of days, and if being reckless let her forget about almost getting shot and finding out it was her fault, well, she'd be reckless.

She squeezed her eyes closed, kissed Russ harder because—damn it—she wanted this. Wanted him.

Don't think.

The condo phone rang. Ignoring it, she wrapped her arms around Russ's neck, pressed her much smaller body into his. Immediately, his arms tightened around her.

The phone kept ringing.

No, no, no.

She leaped back, pushing Russ away and holding her arms straight out. Her breaths came in huge bursts as she stared at his face, all lean angles and dark eyes and—*oh, my*—he was amazing. "I can't believe I'm doing this, but that might be the doorman. No one ever calls the landline anymore."

Russ rubbed his hands over his face. "We're in trouble here."

"I know."

The phone stopped ringing. Missed it. The sudden silence, all that quiet going on outside her rioting brain, didn't offer any comfort. Somehow, it only added to the bedlam. She needed something. Anything to slow her down, because maybe it was a wrong number—please let it have been that—and she and Russ could pick up that blazing kiss exactly where it had left off. His eyes were on her—*he's not running*—and she took a step toward him.

Music sounded from her cell phone. He'd given it back to her once they'd returned to the city. Doorman's ringtone. So much for the wrong number. "Unbelievable, my life." She dug the phone from her purse and hit the button. "Hi, Henry."

"Good evening. Sorry to disturb you so late. I have a United States marshal here to see you."

And Penny laughed. She'd bet Henry didn't get to say that too often. She glanced back at Russ still focused on her with the intensity that, from the first time she'd seen it, rocked her.

Later.

They'd finish it later.

"Thank you, Henry." She disconnected, tossed the phone on the coffee table and tried not to be disappointed when Russ adjusted himself, got everything sort of in order. So to speak. "The other marshal is here."

"I figured."

"I wanted—"

Russ stuck his hand up. "Let's not. No point." He dropped his head back, stared at the ceiling and breathed before bringing his gaze back to her. "We need to focus on the case."

"I know."

Because she never wanted to wear the label of ineffective counsel.

A soft knock sounded and Russ pushed his shoulders back, headed for the door. Without a peephole to check who stood on the other side, he stopped before opening it. "Who is it?"

"Marshal Danson."

Russ cracked the door, hesitated, then stepped back. An extremely un-Brent average-size man entered and flashed his badge at Penny. He didn't look much older than her—maybe early thirties—but his blond hair had already gone gray at the temples. Stress of the job? Who knew?

Russ held his hand out to Danson. "I'm Russ Voight. This is Penny Hennings."

The marshal nodded. "Ma'am."

"She should be good for the night. Just watch the door. I'll be by in the morning to pick her up."

"Got it."

Russ turned to Penny. "You okay?"

So not okay. Because truly, she did not want him walking out the door. *Gummy bears.* A hard, determined edge appeared on his face and his slightly narrowed eyes warned her not to go there. Not in front of the marshal.

"I'm good. Thank you…for everything."

"I'll see you in the morning. Sleep well."

If he thought that would happen, the man was delusional.

Chapter Six

At 9:00 a.m. sharp, Russ followed Penny—once again looking snazzy in stilettos and a suit the color of a perfect summer sky—into her father's big-shot office, where he sat behind his big-shot desk with his feet propped up. Only an insanely rich guy would wear four-thousand-dollar suits, complete with suspenders and a pocket square, and then prop his feet on a desk that probably cost twenty grand.

Across from him in one of the leather desk chairs sat Penny's older brother Zac, who spun around, saw Russ and stood to shake his hand. The guy didn't look too happy to have been summoned.

A *bleep-bleep* sounded from the desk phone. "I have David for you." A woman's voice—probably the secretary.

David Hennings, Penny's oldest brother and—*fantastic*—another lawyer. At least David wasn't a criminal attorney. He'd gone for civil law, but still, a meeting with four lawyers? Russ would rather tackle rattlesnakes.

"Thank you, Margaret." Gerald set his hand on the phone's keypad, then glanced up. "Good morning, Agent Voight."

"Morning, sir."

"Hello, Zachary," Penny said, leaning down to kiss her brother on the cheek.

She offered Russ the guest chair, but he waved her into it.

"I'll stand." If he wanted to sit, he'd take a squat on the overstuffed sofa that was big enough for King Kong to sleep on.

The phone rang and Gerald hit a button. "David?"

"Hi, Dad."

"Hey, Dave," Zac said.

Penny remained quiet. And when the hell had Russ ever experienced that phenomenon?

"Will someone please tell me what is going on?" David said, his voice sharp enough to chop wood.

Ho-kay.

Penny sat forward, moving closer to the phone. "I'm sorry I didn't call you yesterday."

"Ya think? I mean, a heads-up would have been nice before a marshal showed up at my office."

Hang on here.

Russ stepped closer to the desk, but Gerald beat him to it. "Watch your tone. Things got hectic. You got what information I had."

"Well, yeah, but once again the drama queen created chaos and we all suffered for it."

Russ looked at Penny, who refused to even glance at him. She kept her focus on the phone, but her cheeks had gone hollow and she looked to be chewing on the inside of them. Apparently, she and David didn't get along.

Zac sighed. "Dave, relax. It's not her fault."

"Right. It never is. I'm in Boston and I can't get away from her drama. And you and Dad let her get away with it. Every time."

In the thirty seconds Russ had known David Hennings, he despised him. Plus, he didn't like his attitude regarding Penny. And if her father and Zac weren't going to deal with that, Russ would. He reached over the desk, picked up the receiver and dropped it back in its cradle. The three occupants in the room went silent. Obviously people didn't hang up on David. Too bad. Someone had to take control. "He'll call back," Russ said.

Zac elbowed Penny's arm. "I like this guy."

"No fooling," she cracked.

Penny stared up at him, her big blue eyes round and, if his guess was right, amused.

Thirty seconds later, David was patched through again. "Did you hang up on me?" he hollered.

"David," Russ said. "This is special agent Russell Voight. I hung up on you. Keep yelling and I'll do it again. Your only purpose in this meeting is to listen."

"Wait—"

"I will not wait. I wasted five minutes of my life listening to you and I can't get those five minutes back. Your sister did not call you yesterday because soon after being threatened by someone who ordered a mass shooting, I confiscated her phone to avoid a killer locating her. I took her to an FBI safe house, where her client, also my very important witness, met us. She called your father using *my* phone and that was the only communication she had with anyone outside of the FBI or the U.S. Marshals' office. If you have any issues with that, speak to me later. Right now, your sister's client is waiting for me and I can't question her without Penny. So, you will shut up and we'll make this quick."

"Russell Voight," Penny said, "I think I love you."

Gerald Hennings laughed at that. And so did Zac. In fact, David seemed to be the only male involved in this conversation who *didn't* have an affection for Penny.

A brief silence ensued and Russ held his hand to Gerald to continue. "David, until the FBI feels the threats against Penny are no longer an issue, we will all be under protection. Beyond that, there's not much to say."

"David," Penny said, "I took a client. That's all. Had I known this would happen, obviously I would have avoided it."

"Whatever, Penny."

Penny threw her hands up. "How is this my fault? You think I sit around all day thinking up ways to annoy you?

Guess what, *David,* everything isn't about you. Shocking as that may be."

"Okay," Russ said, "I think we're done here." He reached over and hung up on David before the war started. He turned to Gerald. "If he calls back, do me a favor and talk him down. I don't have time for family squabbles now. Besides, he's being unreasonable." He looked at Zac. "Sorry about the inconvenience, but it's for your own safety. For the time being, vary your pattern."

"No Starbucks before work," Penny said. She glanced at Russ. "He stops there every morning."

"She's right. Whatever your normal routine is, change it up. Let's not make it easy for this lunatic."

"Can you get this guy?" Zac wanted to know.

"Yes. As long as your sister's client cooperates, we'll put him away."

Gerald's phone *bleep-bleeped* again. David probably. And David could shove it.

"I have a Colin Heath for Penny," the secretary said. "She wanted me to let her know when he called."

Russ swung to Penny, who stared at the phone as if it had grown fangs.

The men in the room glanced at Penny, then to Russ. "Take it," he said. "Just like we talked about. Got it?"

"Oh, I've got it."

PENNY SCOOPED UP the phone the second it rang. "Hello, Mr. Heath. Punctual, I see."

"When it comes to beautiful women, I try."

She rolled her eyes. What more could she do? She'd like to flip him off, but certain things she wouldn't do in front of her father. Still, psycho or not, Colin Heath probably had a way with women. Just not this woman.

"I've a busy day, so let's make this fast. I'll agree to your terms, Mr. Heath. But I want a guarantee from you—

whatever that might be worth—that Elizabeth and her son will stay safe."

"You'll convince her not to testify?"

"Do I have a choice?"

"Not really."

I'll get you another way, you rat. "Then she won't testify."

"And what will you do about the FBI?"

Penny glanced at Russ and he rolled his hand. "That's my problem to deal with."

"You get the FBI off my tail, Ms. Hennings, and Elizabeth will be safe. After all, her husband made me a lot of money."

Sick, twisted bastard.

"Are we through?"

"We are. I'll be in touch to make sure our deal is going according to plan."

Penny hung up without bothering to say goodbye. Why give him any pleasantries?

Her father leaned forward, stretched his hand to her. "Are you all right?"

"I'm fine, Dad." She squeezed his hand, hoping to reassure him and maybe herself. "It's the right decision."

"Sis," Zac said, "you've got guts."

She shrugged. "Sometimes."

Russ jerked his chin toward the door. "We should go. I still have Brent's car. Sooner we get to Elizabeth, the sooner this case gets wrapped up."

"Of course. Let me grab my laptop."

She hugged her brother, then her father. "I'm sorry about David."

Dad kissed her head the way he used to when she was seven and had suffered some trauma that only Daddy could fix. Even now, all these years later, it mattered.

"I'll handle him."

"Thank you, Dad."

At least she had his and Zac's support.

Downstairs, she stood in the foyer leading to the back alley of the Hennings & Solomon building, waiting for Russ to give her the all clear. The man had a gracefulness about him. Rugged grace. That was what he had. He moved swiftly, his strides purposeful and without hesitation. She imagined him this way all the time. As if an inherent part of him never let up, never stopped pursuing, never appeared weak. Even if he felt it, he'd never show it. Maybe some women were bothered by that. Penny? Not. She herself had trouble admitting her weaknesses and she certainly didn't want to discuss them. Nothing doing there.

Everyone felt weak occasionally. She knew this. Despite the outward appearance, she supposed most humans, on some deep level, hid vulnerabilities. Her brother constantly blamed her for whatever infractions plagued them. It was always Penny's fault. Always.

Russ Voight had just saved her from David's condescension. That alone made her a little gooey.

He opened the alley door, waved her through and got her settled into Brent's government-issued sedan before sliding into the driver's side. "All set?"

"Yes. Oh. My phone." She dug it out of her bag, pulled the battery and dumped the pieces back into her purse. "Now we're set."

"So, David?" Russ said. "Hell of a guy."

She waggled her head. "He's what many would call a real jerk. And I say that with all the love my heart can hold for my brother who hasn't given me a break since the day I popped out of my mother."

Russ turned out of the alley, bullied his way into morning traffic and headed south as the sun bounced off the shiny glass of the Hennings & Solomon building. "What's his problem?"

"Besides the fact that my very existence is somehow my fault, I really couldn't tell you." She caught the lump in her throat, swallowed it back. *Damned David.* Always demoralizing her.

"Why is he in Boston?"

"He moved there four years ago. He's a civil-litigation lawyer and claimed he needed space to do his own thing. My guess is he saw Zac about to take off in his career and my dad had already promised me a spot at the firm."

"Which specializes in criminal defense."

"Yes. Family dinner conversations inevitably turned to current criminal cases in the media and, well, I think David didn't know how he fit in."

"He felt left out?"

She shrugged. "That and there's his ever-growing dislike of *moi.*"

"He's your brother. He has to like you."

Russ glanced at her, twisted those fab lips of his, and something warm and comforting and oh-so-good curled around her. The man was a giant white gummy bear.

"He may love me, but he doesn't like me. And his behavior certainly reflects that, because I only hear from him when he wants to yell at me."

"Come on. Seriously? Does he call Zac?"

Ah, yes, the other constant reminder that her oldest brother saw her as the lesser sibling. "Every two weeks."

"Nice. I can see why you think he has a problem with you."

She finally looked at him. "Thank you, by the way. I nearly wet myself when you hung up on him. That might be the best gift anyone has ever given me."

Russ shrugged. "He was being ignorant. We don't have time for that. I half expect him to call me on it. Not sure I'd mind, either. Sounds to me like your brother needs someone to rip into him."

She swung herself sideways. "Is it wrong that I'm glad he lives in Boston?"

"Honey, I'm thinking he should move overseas."

Penny cracked up. The man she'd decimated on the stand somehow understood the complexities of her relationship with her brother and didn't judge her for her less-than-loving thoughts.

"He makes me feel rotten about myself. Sometimes I believe him and I hate that, but he's still my brother. He's entitled to feel how he feels."

Russ jumped onto the Dan Ryan and hit the gas. Wow. Fast driver. She hadn't noticed that before.

"What stinks," he said, "is it takes him making you feel bad to make himself feel good. Seems cowardly to me, but what do I know? I'm an only child."

You know a lot. She took in the fact that after one brief conversation, Special Agent Voight had basically profiled her brother. And he'd hit his target dead-on. "I didn't picture you as an only child."

"Yeah, me and the folks."

"Do they live here?"

He shifted lanes and bolted past a slower driver. Apparently FBI agents didn't concern themselves with a thing called the speed limit. "Florida. They moved there a few years ago. My dad wanted to retire."

"Was he in law enforcement?"

"No. He's a mechanic."

Again, something she'd never imagined. For whatever reason—perhaps his confidence or sense of self—she pictured him growing up in a household with a man in uniform. Damned Russell Voight making her so interested in him. "So, why the FBI for you, then?"

THAT SLURPING NOISE was Russ getting sucked into a vacuum. Only problem was, he liked getting sucked in. Specifically, he liked it with Penny, which brought his male mind to places it should definitely not be going.

How much he should admit here, he wasn't sure. Typically, he didn't open up to women about his childhood. And he'd never done it with a defense attorney. Male or female. Which, yeah, was creating issues, because when alone with Penny, he saw her as good company. Good female company with a nice compact body he'd like to have under him at some point. These thoughts didn't mesh with this case and prosecuting Colin Heath for the lives he'd ruined. Pump-and-dump scheme aside, he wanted to pin him with the murder of that reporter on the courthouse steps. What kind of psycho threatened someone by terrorizing hundreds of people? Since becoming an FBI agent, he'd asked himself that question no less than a thousand times and the answer continued to elude him.

"Russell?"

Now or never. He could put her off. Tell her he wanted to help people who'd been wronged, which wouldn't be a lie.

Also wouldn't be the truth.

"When I was twelve our house went into foreclosure."

"I'm so sorry."

"Some mortgage scammer convinced my dad they'd buy the loan from the bank and charge my folks a lower interest rate. My dad is no fool. He asked around about the guy and he checked out."

"Oh, no."

He glanced at her and found her studying him. Focused. He loved that about her. Her ability to concentrate wholly on her subject. "The scammer duped hundreds of people out of their homes. When the bank came calling, looking for the twelve months of payments my folks paid to the scammer, the guy disappeared. My dad was never the same after that. He never said, but I think it made him feel like less of a man. A man who couldn't support his family. I could see it. He changed."

"And that's why you like working financial frauds?"

Russ shrugged. "There's personal satisfaction in it. I wish I could find the guy. I'm sure he's still running scams."

"Have you searched for him?"

A trooper had parked on the shoulder and Russ cruised by him doing eighty-five. *Whoops.* He waved and hoped to hell the guy recognized a government-issued car. When the trooper stayed put, Russ went back to Penny. "Every month I look for him. He'll turn up. Guys like him can't stay away. It's like crack to them. The next scam. The next con. They get off on it."

"How about your parents? Did they get back on their feet?"

"They did, but it took years. Their credit was shot. Couldn't get a mortgage and rented for fifteen years. My dad broke his back saving money so he could pay cash for the house in Florida. He never wanted another mortgage."

"Is this why you hate defense attorneys? Because we defend scammers?"

He glanced at her and wondered how the hell he could even pretend to dislike her. Smart, sexy and unafraid. "It's not my favorite profession." He cracked a grin, then went back to the road. "After that smoking kiss last night, you're the exception to my rule."

"Oh, *Russell.* You're so good to me."

If he'd doubted it before, he now knew he was whacked out over Penny Hennings. "Do we need to talk about it? Last night?"

She shifted front again. "Nope. Won't do us any good. Other than to torture me."

Ain't seen nothing yet, babe. "There are things I would like to do to you. They require a flat surface. Preferably a soft one."

From his peripheral vision, he saw her crack the window.

"You'll have to wait, though. I'm not blowing this case because I'm fantasizing about you naked. Except for a pair of stilettos—the red ones from the other day—and that pink bra from last night."

"Oh, please. That would be so uncomfortable. You really have no idea. Not to mention they don't match."

"Certain times, I don't care about comfort or fashion."

She laughed. "Then I guess we'll have to find Colin Heath in a hurry."

"I'm on it. We're chasing down every known contact he has. We'll get him. He can't hide forever."

Chapter Seven

By midafternoon, Penny needed a double-shot latte and some white gummy bears on the side. Russ had been hammering away at Elizabeth for hours, and the woman, despite minor memory lapses and exhaustion, held up remarkably well.

After hours of killing time in his room, Sam had been allowed to play in the yard. The little rascal then moved to convincing his marshal he should be allowed by the lakefront. At which point, the kid argued that his mother had buzzed his hair the night before and if he wore a baseball cap and glasses, he'd be incognito. All around, the wrong life for a child, but no one seemed to disagree with his logic. Hopefully, Penny could get them a different life, where they'd both be free to wander outdoors without fear.

Russ jotted a note, then looked back at Elizabeth. "Did your husband seem off? Stressed?"

"Yes," Elizabeth said. "When I asked him about it, he said Colin was putting a lot of pressure on him. He wouldn't elaborate. Two weeks later, my husband was dead."

"And when did Heath come to you and ask you to start doing the trades so he could keep the scam going?"

"Maybe two weeks after Sam's death. That's when I truly understood what my husband had been involved in. According to Colin, the investors were calling, wanting their money. Colin didn't have it. He told me I'd have to make trades. He wanted the stock price to go up and then he'd convince the investors to stay in the deal. He planned on bringing in new investors to cover the trades he wanted me to do."

"To pump up the price?"

"Yes."

"You made the trades?"

"When he threatened my son, yes."

"Maybe it's time for a break," Penny said.

Russ dropped his pen, sat back and stretched his arms across the back of the sofa, pulling the material of his dress shirt snug against his chest.

Oh, boy. Something told Penny the special agent had a rocking bod under all that FBI wear.

"I'm not judging you," he said. "I'm taking information. Besides, I'd have done it. I'd imagine most parents would."

I'm going to jump him. She didn't know when or particularly how, but as of this second, Russell Voight would now be the only name on her I-must-have-him list.

Time for some air. Penny stood. "Break time! I know I need one and nobody speaks without me here, so there you go. Sugar right now would be exceptional. Russell? Anything in this place contain copious amounts of sugar?"

Still with his arms stretched across the sofa and studying her with an idle curiosity that sparked heat in naughty places, he jerked his chin toward the kitchen. "Pantry. We stocked up on cookies for Sam. Brent, too."

"Dude," Brent said, and Russ laughed.

The good-natured fun eased the tension in the room and Penny shook her head in mock disgust.

"I like cookies," Brent said. "So what?"

Russ held his hands up. "I was just making a statement."

"You were throwing shade, man. I'm not ashamed that I like cookies."

"Relax, boys. I'll make a pot of coffee to go with our

cookies. I hope it's not those disgusting processed cookies. We need bakery cookies."

"*Bakery* cookies?" Russ shot back.

"Hey. If you're going to eat cookies, they might as well be worth the calories." Penny squatted in front of Elizabeth. "You holding up okay? Can I get you anything?"

She stared at the window frame, where sunshine slipped through the edge of the blind that blocked the spectacular lake view. Maybe what they *all* needed was air. "Russell, Elizabeth and I are going outside for a few minutes."

"Why?"

Uh, my client is tired.

"I need to confer with my client."

He stood. "Do it here. I'll give you privacy."

"No. We'll go outside. How do I know if this place is bugged?"

His head dipped forward. "You've got to be kidding."

"Last I checked? No."

A muscle in his jaw flexed and those dark eyes turned hard, unyielding. Even with the camaraderie they'd built, she couldn't resist reminding the FBI agent she had a responsibility to her client.

"Fine," he said. "Go. Ten minutes. Keep her out of sight."

Penny led Elizabeth through the kitchen to the back door, where she waited for a frowning Brent to exit ahead of them. The men didn't seem to like her idea of going outside. They'd have to suck it up.

Brent checked the perimeter, then waved them through. "Stay close to the house."

"Will do. And thank you."

Elizabeth followed Penny down the curving brick steps to the patio, where Penny stopped and stared out at the lake. Hot today, but the sun and the lake made her think of family outings from her childhood. Even back then, before her father had made his name, before they could afford a vacation home, her parents had loved visiting the lake. Someday, she'd do just as her father had done and buy herself a lake home. Something small. A cottage she could add on to. Maybe put a growing family in.

Beside her, Elizabeth waggled her fingers in front of Penny. "What is it?"

"What?"

"What do you need to talk to me about?"

"Nothing. I thought you could use some air. The questions are tough."

Elizabeth gave her a small but grateful smile. "Thank you. But I knew what I was getting into."

"Penny?" Russ called from the porch doorway.

It hadn't been a minute and a half and he was bothering them already? He'd promised privacy. "Russell, it's barely been two minutes."

He held out his phone. "It's your secretary."

Her phone was still off and currently in her purse—minus the battery—so any important calls were being funneled through Russ. She supposed she couldn't be irritated with him, since he obviously didn't mind playing messenger boy.

"Thank you. Sorry to bug you with my calls."

She grabbed the phone, but he held it a second while her fingers brushed his and that same spark snapped between them. She lingered for the shortest time measurable, but it could have been an hour. He knew his power. Which made it all the more fun for her.

"It's not a problem," he said, grinning like a madman.

She rolled her eyes and laughed. The man irritated her, but he also made her smile. She snatched the phone from him and shooed him away. "Hi, Margaret."

"Hi. I hate to tell you this, but your building manager just called. You left your tub running this morning."

Ridiculous. "I didn't."

"He said you did. Water poured through your downstairs neighbor's ceiling."

Suddenly, Russ poked his head out the door again, but she focused on Margaret. “Well, I’m sure that is, but it’s not from my place. I haven’t taken a bath in ten years.”

Silence. Maybe her hot-water heater burst? What a mess that would be.

Penny shook it off. “I’ll call the building manager. Did he leave a number? I can’t get to it on my phone.”

Margaret rattled off the number and Penny repeated it to herself. “Thanks.”

Russ came back onto the porch. “What’s up?”

“Hang on. I don’t want to forget this number.”

Before hitting Send, she looked up at Russ on the steps, the afternoon sun drenching him in bright light. She wanted to be here with him, enjoying the sunshine without a case sitting between them.

“My building manager called. They think my tub overflowed. Which—hello?—is impossible because I don’t take baths. Why would anyone enjoy sitting in dirty water? Ick.”

She hit Send and waited for the building manager, a cranky guy named Morton who was older than God.

“Hello?”

“Hello, Morton. This is Penny Hennings.”

“Hi, Penny. Listen. Big problem. Your tub overflowed and went through the floor. Made a hell of a mess.”

“Have you checked my apartment?”

“We did. Had to go in to shut the water off. We tried your cell but it went to voice mail.”

She glanced up at Russ. Not that he could be blamed, but she needed her phone. The thing was like oxygen and Russ was stepping on the tube. “How bad is the damage?” she asked the building manager.

“Your bathroom and outer hall are soaked. Carpet will have to come up and you’ll probably need to replace drywall. Helluva mess.”

“Morton, I don’t see how that’s possible. I don’t use

the tub and I certainly wouldn't have forgotten to turn the shower off."

"Saw it myself. The water was on full blast and the tub stopper was in. If you didn't leave it on, someone did."

Chapter Eight

By the time they'd arrived at Penny's building, a team of FBI agents had cleared the premises in case her intruder was idiot enough to hide in one of her closets.

Intruder. Right. She knew who it was. Even before she'd stepped through the front door, she knew.

Now she stood in the elevator, flanked by Russ and Brent, impatiently waiting to reach her floor. The elevator doors slid open and Russ blocked her with his arm before sticking his head out. "We clear?"

"You're good," a female voice said from down the hall.

A female FBI agent. Very cool. Penny shoved around Russ, who grunted at her. "*Russell,* she just said it's clear. I should be allowed to see my own house."

The female agent standing in the hallway dipped her head in greeting. "Ma'am."

The woman was too darned close to Penny's age to be calling her ma'am. On a good day, she'd have made a smart-mouthed comment. On a good day. "May I go in?"

"Hey, Cathy," Russ said from behind her.

A sudden burst of heat shot up Penny's neck. Something in the way he said the woman's name—slow, *familiar*—caught her attention and she angled back to Russ. His eyes were on the apartment door. Not the woman. She swung back to Cathy, who met her gaze for a split second before turning front. Russ kept his eyes glued to the door.

Are you kidding me?

He'd slept with this woman. How she knew it, she had no idea, but the guilt—or discomfort—was evident by the way Russ refused to make eye contact with either one of them.

Penny shoved open the door. "Russell Voight, you are totally killing me."

"What?"

"Oh, please." But damn him. She didn't want to think about him in bed with the pretty, *busty* brunette at the door. Penny didn't have boobs. Well, she had them, of course, but they weren't enough to fill a man's hand. They were barely enough to fill her padded A cup.

Men. Pigs.

"Booties," Cathy said.

Penny shot her a look. "Pardon?"

"We're treating this as a crime scene. You need booties and gloves."

She pointed at the two boxes on the floor. One contained those silly paper shoe coverings servicemen slipped on to avoid getting the carpet dirty when they came to the house. The other held gloves.

"I'll wait out here," Brent said. "No sense trampling a crime scene. Holler if you need me."

Penny kicked off her shoes and slipped on the booties. Joke, that. They barely stayed on her miniscule feet. Story of her life. Too small for just about everything.

The gloves came next. Behind her, Russ went through the same routine and she tried not to act like an ice queen, but found it irrationally hard. He and Cathy had slept together. Big deal. People did it all the time. Workplace shenanigans. It happened.

Only, she was never jealous before and that was what this was. It might have been tough to admit, but she'd never been accused of being in denial. Nope. Penny Hennings called it as she saw it. Even when she wished she hadn't seen whatever she supposedly saw.

Inside the apartment, two male agents dressed in suits—the standard FBI look—stood in her kitchen, probably to avoid the soaked carpet.

"ERT is still in the bathroom," one of the agents said to Russ.

"Thanks." He held Penny's arm to keep her from marching toward the bathroom. "What's with the attitude?"

What did he expect? First her home was invaded and now she had to deal with the pretty FBI agent that Russ, a man she'd allowed herself the luxury of lusting after, most likely slept with.

"Forget it. None of my business. I need to see what I'm dealing with here."

Russ twisted his lips and his gaze shot over her face, checking her features for any tell. He retreated a few steps to the kitchen opening. "Guys, give us a second."

"Sure thing, Russ."

The two men filed out and Russ locked the door behind them. He met her in the hallway, glanced over her shoulder toward the closed bathroom door, then folded his arms. "Spill it."

Heat flooded her cheeks. How the heck could she say this without embarrassing herself? *I can't.* She had no right to be jealous. Not even a smidge of a right. They were nothing to each other. They'd shared a steamy kiss, sure, but they weren't an item.

Water from the soaked carpet sloshed under her feet and she stared down at it. Colin Heath—or someone he'd sent—had to have done this. Somehow, they'd gotten past the doorman or her gated garage and entered her apartment.

"I slept with her," Russ said.

Penny closed her eyes and heaved out a breath. Somehow, she didn't need that confirmation. Oh, but she'd known. "It's not my business."

"Well, you're royally ticked at me for whatever it is I did in the hallway."

"You didn't do anything. That's the problem. It was your voice, and then you wouldn't make eye contact."

"It was one night two years ago. She wasn't even assigned to my office at the time. We had fun, and that was it. I swear to you."

She stared up at him, watched his eyes. No movement. Just a steady focus on hers. *He's not lying.* He could have been lying. Some people were that good at it. When he chose to lie, Russ was probably one of those people. Right now, looking into his eyes, she didn't think this was the case now.

"You don't owe me explanations."

"Yeah, I do. I don't want you thinking I make a habit of sleeping with coworkers."

"Now I know." It still hurt, though, and she smacked him on the chest. "Damn you."

"I told the truth!"

"And what am I supposed to do with that? I don't want to feel this way about you." She flapped her arms. "You're like a giant white gummy bear. All sweet and sugary and satisfying."

At that, he grinned and she could have cracked him again. This time harder. Just one punch that he wouldn't expect from Miss Puny but that Zac had taught her how to deliver. A punch from her would knock that grin off his face.

"You're jealous."

"Oh, stop it, Russell. I've had a rotten few days." She threw her hands out. "Now this. Someone bypassed all the supposed security precautions and marched right in. Why? Because I agreed to his terms. I did everything he wanted and he's still at it."

"He wants you to know he's still watching."

"That he can get to me, right?"

Russ scratched the back of his neck and ran his hand into his hair. "Yeah. That's my guess."

"So, if I double-cross him, this is my way of knowing he can to do to me what he did to Sam Brooks." She slapped her hands on her head. "I can't believe this. I'm an attorney. This shouldn't happen to me."

Russ held his hands up. "Hang on. Let's deal with one thing at a time. The evidence guys need to finish up in here."

She stared at the powder smudges on the entry door. "I see that. You can't believe Heath would have left fingerprints. This place is probably spotless. And it's contaminated anyway because the building manager came in."

No response. He knew she was right.

"You need to make sure nothing is missing."

She poked him in the chest. "I'll bet you a hundred dollars there's not one thing out of place. He came in here for the purpose of letting me know he was here. And you know what really infuriates me?"

He grabbed her poking finger and gently squeezed. "Aside from all of it?"

"Yes. What really makes me crazy is how the hell this man knew I didn't take baths." A sob caught in her throat—*What is that?* She swallowed, forcing it down, beating it into submission.

"What are you talking about?"

"I haven't taken a bath in ten years. Either this guy got seriously lucky by coming in here and randomly running a bath or—"

"Or he knows you don't take baths and therefore you would know that someone who had that information got into your house."

"Exactly."

Russ walked to the front door, opened it and checked the lock.

"No forced entry," one of the agents outside said.

Russ stepped into the hallway, glanced in all directions, then came back in. "Are there security cameras in the hallway?"

"No. Only at the street level. Check the gate. That thing

is so slow anyone can scoot under it. I've complained a thousand times."

"We're on it already. Trust me, we'll see how this guy got in here."

Russ stood, shoulders back, hands on hips, his fingers twitching against the fabric of his pants. From three feet away she felt it. All that contained energy he fought to control. That need to do something and do it now.

Nothing like a man who knew how to take charge of a situation.

Having put the battery back into her phone the second they'd hit the city limits, Penny's cell rang. She checked the number—blocked—then snapped her gaze to Russ. "It's blocked. Heath always calls from a blocked number."

"Answer it."

Gladly. Time to put this guy in his place. Stop being the victim. "Hello, Mr. Heath."

"Ah, you know it's me?"

"Don't let it go to your head. So, now that you've flooded my apartment, I'm guessing you'll pay for the damage?"

Heath laughed and it was one of those soft, only slightly amused chuckles that got on her nerves. "Something funny?"

"Nothing at all, actually. I see you're spending time with the FBI."

Penny glanced at Russ. They'd been so careful about smuggling her in and out of alleys and having her slide down in her seat until Russ had been sure they weren't followed.

Someone's inside.

"I'm a defense lawyer, Mr. Heath. I have a lot of cases. Plenty of them involve the FBI."

"Coincidence that it's Special Agent Voight. The one handling Elizabeth Brooks."

"Agent Voight has multiple cases, as well. How'd you get into my home?"

Heath sighed. "With the right resources, it's easy enough."

Through the phone, a siren sounded. Penny cocked her head. *In stereo.* She walked to the window, pulled the phone from her ear and heard a siren from the street below.

He's here.

A million tiny tingles zapped her arms. *Here. Here. Here.* She charged to the desk, where she scribbled a note to Russ. "Oh, I'll figure it out," she said into the phone.

Maybe sooner than you think.

Russ read the note, glanced up at her and mouthed, *Keep him talking.*

He sprinted to the door and threw it open. He'd better hurry, because there was only so much small talk she could muster with a man who wanted nothing more than to terrorize her. To bend her to his will. As if she'd ever allow that.

"So, is this a social call? Just enough for you to let me know you're watching me."

"I know every step you make, lovely Penny. The tub was your first warning. Stop talking to the FBI."

A horn sounded and then there were only voices. *Moved inside.* She resisted peering out the window. If he was that close, he might see her. Where the hell was he? And then the singing started and her head nearly exploded from the raging blood rush. *I know that song.*

Gotcha.

The idiot had stepped into the ice-cream shop across the street. Little did Mr. Heath know that the employees, upon receiving a tip, broke into song.

Penny scribbled another note, rushed to the door as she spoke. "Mr. Heath, I've told you, I have other business with the FBI. I made a deal with you. I won't go back on that deal."

The man was right across the street. She'd give him credit for one thing and that was having a spine. He threatened her, broke into her home, flooded the place and then stood on the street outside watching the action.

Sneaky SOB.

She swung the door open and passed the note to Cathy, the-woman-who-slept-with-Russ-first. She nodded, yanked her phone from her belt, and Penny closed the door.

"I know you won't go back on that deal," he said. "The tub was insurance. I've got you, Penny. I see everything."

The slam of a car door came through the phone line. Moving again.

Get there, Russ. Please.

"This will be my last warning, Penny. Whatever you're talking to the FBI about, stop."

Get there, Russ. She paced the room. *Stall. Figure something out. Do something.*

"How am I supposed to do that? I've promised you I'd make this happen and I will."

Pause. Where was he? *To hell with it.* She peeked out the window just as Russ darted across the street. "Hello?"

"Oh, Penny. You've just made a serious mistake."

RUSS BOLTED INTO TRAFFIC and nearly got mauled by a car trying to catch the amber. At least he'd ditched the damned booties and could move faster. Two men stood in front of the ice-cream shop Cathy had just told him Heath called from.

The guy in a white shirt and a blue baseball cap talked on his cell, spotted Russ and moved around the corner. The second guy, that one in jeans and a polo shirt, cut away and went the other direction.

Decision time.

From Russ's distance and the similar builds of the men, he couldn't decipher which was Heath. Which one to follow? *Who, who, who?*

Ball cap.

Heath would try to hide under it. Russ swung around the corner, blew by a woman in a stroller and nearly knocked a businessman on his tail. Still, he kept his eyes on his unsub sprinting to the opposite end of the block. Heath. Had to be. *Go, go, go.*

He hit the button on the radio Cathy had handed him. "Corner of North Sheridan. Blue baseball cap. Denim cargo shorts. White shirt. White shirt! North Sheridan!"

Heath bolted into the street, running diagonally. A car slammed its brakes and got nailed by the car behind. *Oofff!* A woman rushed from a store to see the action—*move*—and Russ skidded around her, bumping a parked car as he spun away from the woman and lost precious time. Damn it. He shot across the street. Ball cap. *Where is it?* There. Turning east.

At a dead run, he hit the corner, and a mob of people getting off the bus blocked his view. *Out of the way. Come on. Come on.* He shoved around them, his gaze sweeping the area, checking building alcoves and store entrances. Nothing.

A whooshing sound came from the bus as it pulled away and—ah, dang it—Russ ran next to the bus, scouring the windows. No blue ball cap.

He spun away from the bus, scanned the area where a cab pulled away from the curb. The back of a guy's head. Brown hair. No ball cap.

Russ glanced in the other direction. *Nada.* He propped his still-gloved hands on his hips and tapped his fingers. *Where'd you go?*

The cab was now halfway down the block and his pulse slammed, his breaths coming in short bursts that he knew better to control. He watched the cab shoot down the street and make a right. Did the guy in the cab have a white shirt on?

Damn it.

He checked the curb. Nothing. Garbage can. Right beside him. He peered inside. Blue ball cap.

Every swearword he knew streamed from his lips. Finally, he bit down until his jaw ached. *Get a grip here.* A pedestrian stepped up to use the trash can. Russ flipped his badge up and waved the woman off before hooking his gloved finger through the back strap on the cap and fishing it out of the garbage. Trash. Fair game. No warrant necessary.

Come to me, DNA.

Chapter Nine

Penny turned when Zac stepped into her apartment dressed in a sharp gray suit and light pink shirt. Had to love her brother for having no issues about wearing a pink shirt. He shut the door behind him, making it clear to the agents outside that they were not welcome to join the conversation. Knowing she'd need someone—specifically Zac, who'd been helping her through any number of situations for years—she'd called him from Russell's phone on the way back to the city.

"What the hell?" he said.

If she'd had any answers, she'd be glad to share, but right now all she knew was this nut Heath seemed to know her every move. She threw her hands up. "This guy is a viper."

Zac spun toward the hallway, but didn't move. Being a prosecutor, he knew enough not to traipse through a crime scene—which was exactly what her apartment was—and destroy possible evidence.

"Where's Russ?"

"Last I saw he was running down the street chasing Heath."

Zac gawked. "Heath was here?"

"He called me. From across the street. He's insane."

Zac rubbed his hand over his face and sighed in a way that reminded her of their father when a case unraveled. "You can't stay here. Stay at Mom and Dad's."

Their parents lived in a gated community outside of the city, so Penny understood her brother's immediate assumption she would be safe there. It might, in fact, not be a bad idea, but what she needed to do was distance herself from her family. If she could do that, maybe they'd stay off Heath's radar. Yes. What she needed was to keep the focus on her.

"You need to go, Zac."

"Why?"

"You can't be here."

"Pffft."

Heaven forbid her brother should listen to her. She marched over to him, grabbed the lapels of his jacket and shoved him. So what if he was a foot taller.

"Don't start, Penny."

"Leave."

"I know what you're doing. Me leaving won't keep this guy from coming after me. Or Mom. Or Dad. He knows your weak spots. He'll take advantage. No matter where we go, if he wants to, he'll find us."

"Zachary!"

But Zac, being Zac, didn't yell back. He simply stood there, staring down at her, his features relaxed. Neutral. Unaccusing.

Finally, he squeezed her arm. "Accept it and plan for it. What's your plan?"

He knew her too well. She narrowed her eyes, hesitated. Of course she had a plan, one she'd hatched while speaking with her tormentor.

Zac rolled his eyes. "Again with the drama?"

"I'm putting an investigator from the firm on Heath. I'm done with him thinking he can control me. I'm not good with that."

"You don't think the feds will take issue on that one?"

"I don't care what they do. I'm a citizen being harassed and they can't seem to locate this man until he's standing ten feet from me. I have a right to hire an independent investigator to find him. How do we know the FBI doesn't have a leak?"

That made Zac laugh. "I do love you, Penny. No fear. That's you. Russ Voight will blow a gasket."

The door flew open and in stepped Russ, his short dark hair a little messy, his tie crooked and sweat pouring down his face. He carried a blue baseball cap.

Russ's gaze shot from Penny to Zac and back. "What gasket?"

Penny scrunched her nose at her brother—who had completely thrown her under the bus without even trying—and contemplated an assault charge. At twelve, he'd taught her how to not punch like a girl and he'd long since regretted it since, she typically used that form of defense on him. *Just one good shot...*

"Hit me," Zac said, "and I'll kill you. Right in front of an FBI agent."

An audible sigh came from said FBI agent, who still held the baseball cap. "Hello? What damned gasket? I don't have time for this."

Penny pointed. "Why are you holding that?"

"It belongs to the guy I was chasing. I'm sending it to the lab. See if we hit on anything. Prints, DNA, anything we can identify him with. Chances are we won't get a good print. Not with the hat's material. Maybe from the plastic on the back. DNA is more likely."

"So, you lost him?"

A murderous glare came her way and Penny stepped back. "I'm just asking."

"Yes. I lost him. He got a good jump on me. There were two of them and they split off. I went with the guy on the phone, thinking he was the one talking to you. I didn't get a look at his face. I think it was Heath."

"Who was the other guy?"

"I don't know. Now, what gasket am I about to blow?"

Penny stepped back another inch and readied herself for Russ's rage. The only way to approach this was head-on. Just lay it out there. "I'm calling in one of the firm's investigators."

"Uh, negative on that."

She tilted her head. "Excuse me?"

"No investigators. They'll screw up my case."

"Well, that's too bad, *Russell.* I can't have Heath taking over my life." She jabbed her finger toward the bathroom. "The man was in my house. And the FBI can't find him."

The door opened again and Brent, booties on his giant feet, stepped in. If the raised voices caused alarm, he didn't show it. Just another day in paradise. He held open a clear plastic evidence bag and Russ dropped the hat into it and sealed it. "Thanks. I'll take care of it."

Brent glanced at Penny. "You okay?"

He might be pushy, but he was a good guy. "I'm fine. Be out in a minute."

He nodded in a way that let her know he'd be close if she needed him. Maybe he and Russ were on the government's side, but Brent was one of those ultra-alphas who made taking care of women an art form. She'd sensed it from the second he'd stepped into her chaotic world. Personality traits such as that were always good to know. He moved out the door again. Penny glanced at Zac leaning against her bookcase with his arms folded. Another alpha she'd pegged long ago. If he thought she was in trouble, he'd jump in. No matter how they fought or disagreed, they always backed each other up.

"Russ," Brent said, "the investigator might not be a bad idea. Maybe a fresh set of eyes would help."

Thank you.

Russ sucked in his cheeks. Thought about it. Or at least pretended to think about it. This man puzzled her. She didn't know him well enough yet to figure out his mannerisms and right now, he had her stumped. Anything could be cooking in that brain of his.

He gave Penny a hard stare and her stomach pitched. "I don't necessarily disagree. But I'm not willing to risk my case. No investigator. Am I clear?"

Is he clear? He did not just say that to her. They were in her apartment, her *trashed* apartment, and he thought he could treat her like an imbecile. Like a hysterical female who needed him to control a situation for her. Ha. "Oh, you've made yourself clear, Special Agent Voight. No doubt about that."

Again, he propped his hands on his hips and tapped his fingers. "I take it from the sarcasm you won't listen."

"I don't like your tone. I'm an attorney, *Russell.* A damned good one and I don't appreciate you treating me like I'm some vapid woman.

"Oh, come on!"

Penny stayed silent. Why argue with someone just as stubborn and bullheaded as herself? No point. Besides, she hadn't agreed to anything. Dirty pool? Maybe. But as long as she didn't agree that she wouldn't put an investigator on this, he couldn't accuse her of going back on her word.

Zac boosted himself off the bookcase. "You two arguing isn't accomplishing much and I need to get back to the office. Everyone cool down and we'll revisit this investigator thing later."

"No revisiting," Russ said, his gaze still on Penny.

Penny turned to her brother. "Go back to work. I'm fine."

She watched her only ally walk out the door, took a breath and swore—*swore*—she would not lose her temper. The only way to battle an overbearing man would be to stay calm. Rational. Not give him any ammunition. She faced Russ again. Breathed deep. *I've got this.* "I understand your feelings. That being said, I'd like to offer a compromise. How about I have my investigator contact you, and you can work together? Private investigators have more *freedom* than federal agents."

"Meaning he can bend the law where he sees fit?"

"I didn't say that."

"But that's what you meant." He stepped closer, crowded her space just enough for her to know it. "And when he bends the law too much and gets evidence thrown out because some hotshot defense lawyer—someone like you—proves Heath's constitutional rights were violated, it could blow my case. No investigator. You gave me your word about working with me on this. I expect you to honor that."

Penny inched forward. Why should she be the only one crowded? "And you told me you'd protect us."

Clearly, Russ didn't know her at all.

And somehow, that hurt. What she expected from him she didn't know, but she wanted his respect. She wanted him to understand she wouldn't allow someone to terrorize her. For whatever reason, it was important to her that he know that. "Hang on—"

"No. The man marched right into my house. I'm supposed to let that go? After he's been in here? Probably sneaking around, pawing through my personal items. I'll have to wash every damned bit of underwear I own just to be rid of the creep factor."

Russ moved even closer, one step that left him just inches from her. His posture had shifted slightly, his shoulders more relaxed. Nonthreatening. Smart man. She stared straight ahead at his tie and the intricate pattern of lines. Instinctively she knew it would be a disaster if she made eye contact with him. He was an FBI agent trained to deal with people. If she looked at him, she'd see warmth and understanding, not the anger from seconds ago.

Don't look at him. Not with all this emotional sludge building up inside her. Dealing with the apartment invasion was one thing; adding her conflicted feelings about Russ left her downright bereft.

And yet, despite the aggression between them, there was something about Russell Voight that settled her, allowed her to be convinced of things she didn't necessarily want to be convinced of. *Giant gummy bear.*

Exactly why she couldn't face him.

"Look at me," he said.

"No."

"Penny."

"No."

He dipped his head a bit. "I know what you're doing. It won't work."

Slowly, she lifted her right hand and—*bam!*—punched him. One good shot midbiceps. The punch skidded off—*darn it*—only to be followed by snoring noises from the FBI agent.

I hate him. Sometimes. Not all the time. She hated him when he got her number. When he maneuvered a conversation to fit his needs.

How mad could she be, since her irritation came from him beating her at her own intellectual game?

Suddenly, the stress of the day, all that emotional upheaval, sucked away her energy reserves—*whoosh*—and she could barely hold her head up. So blasted tired.

Not knowing what else to do, she leaned forward and rested her forehead against his chest. *Weak.* "I can't look at you."

She closed her eyes and breathed in the raw, male scent of him. He set his hands on her arms and slid them up and down, creating heat and awareness and—wow—he was close. A low squeeze in her belly consumed her.

Step back.

"Talk to me, Penny."

And still, she stood there, breathing in his scent, letting her aching body recover from her atrocious day. "No. You'll talk me out of the investigator. I know it. And I don't want to be talked out of it. This man terrifies me. I hate that

I've allowed him to do this to me and I really hate that I'm willing to let you talk me out of it."

Total failure.

Finally, he set her back, propped his finger under her chin and pushed up. She let him do it, but kept her eyes closed.

"I need you to trust me. Please. I'll take care of you. We'll get this guy."

Finally, she opened her eyes. "It's not you I don't trust. It's him."

"Understandable. Putting one of your investigators on this will only give him more power. Take the power back, Penny. He knows you love the battle. This is exactly what he expects you to do. He's playing you, and you're letting him."

"I am not."

"He expects you to fight back. Maybe he doesn't know how you'll do it, but he's waiting for you to engage. Don't. Make him wonder. This scenario stinks of a guy who's scared. He knows something is up. He wants you to panic. People make mistakes when they panic. Don't let him manipulate you."

Oh, oh, oh. He had to be kidding with *that* one. *Whatever.*

"You can't believe I'll fall for that?"

He shrugged. "What?"

"Oh, puh-lease, Russell. You're totally baiting me with that don't-let-him-manipulate-you line. You want me to agree with you."

"Of course I do. Why else would I be standing here?"

At that, she laughed. As annoying as he was, she might love this man. She poked him in the chest. Hard. "Here's the deal. I'll play it your way. For now. If that turns out bad—" she twirled her finger and poked him again "—we revisit it. That's as far as I'll go. Be happy with it and accept the deal."

He laughed. "You make me crazy."

"I know."

"But it's a good crazy that gives me some kind of twisted enjoyment. Frankly, it's a hassle. You're tough and beautiful and insanely argumentative, and the whole damn package is scorching hot. You challenge me in ways I don't want to be challenged, but I'd like to compromise. I want you safe and feeling at least somewhat comfortable. Within reason, I'm open to your ideas on how to do that."

"Except for the investigator."

"Except for the investigator. That, I can't do. It's too risky. And you need to promise me you won't do it. You may not believe me, but I know you. If you say it to me, I know you'll keep your word. It's when you're quiet I don't trust you."

She could cross her fingers—as childish as that was—and say it. Then put the investigator on it until something came up and she had to admit it to Russ. At which point, any faith he had, any trust they'd built, would be destroyed.

Or she could say it and mean it and hope that special agent Russell Voight, being the exemplary investigator she knew him to be, could catch their suspect. A man who took perverse pleasure in seeing her weakened.

Russ's gaze met hers, those dark eyes laser sharp, searching for any sign of deception. *He'll know.* She nodded. "No investigators. I promise."

He grinned. All manly I-have-won and she curled her fingers into a fist, ready to strike. "Don't you dare gloat. I will hurt you." She shook her fist at him. "I will bring you so much pain that you'll walk out of here wondering how it happened."

But he kept grinning and inching forward until they were toe-to-toe, bodies so close that she felt his breath on her face. *Total gummy bear.*

"Thank you," he said.

He dipped his head and kissed her. Gently. A slow slide of his lips, barely a caress, and the softness looped inside her, filled her. So warm. She strung her arms around his neck and pulled him closer, wanting full contact, all that body heat transferring into her, washing away the cold ache that came with the day's events.

He eased his hands around her waist, down to the small of her back and held her for a second. And still, his lips were soft on hers. No hurried rush like last time, and it felt good and right and perfect. An unspoken promise that there'd be more, just not right now.

That was okay. She liked this. Liked the dual sides of Russell Voight and the surprises he brought to her.

She backed away, smoothed the lapel of his jacket. "We should stop. Last time we did this, we agreed that we need to concentrate on the case."

He flopped his bottom lip out. "Way to kill a great moment, counselor."

"I know. I'm just not sure which one of us I'm trying to convince."

Chapter Ten

Russ glanced up from his paperwork and stared at Joel Kellogg, a member of one of the Chicago field office's four evidence response teams. The Chicago ERTs consisted of ten special agents dispatched to crime scenes to gather evidence. At well over six feet, Joel was known around the office as the Geek Giant. The man loved all things geek-related and relished the order and demands of evidence collection.

"Processed that hat," Joel said. "Got a print off the plastic tab on the back. Your guy has a record longer than my arm."

"Heath?"

"No."

Who the hell were they talking about? He was so sure it had been Heath. "Who, then?"

"This guy's name is Randolph—aka Randy—Jones. Thirty-four years old, grew up in Evanston. He's done time twice. Once for robbery. Once for aggravated kidnapping."

Russ whistled. "Class X felony. Minimum six years."

"He served eight for snatching up his ex-girlfriend and trying to convince her to take him back. Part of his convincing meant beating her. A neighbor heard the yelling and called the cops. Prior to that he did three years for robbery. Guy has been in and out of prison since he was nineteen."

At the very least, this was someone who had no problem hurting women. Penny's perfect face flashed in Russ's mind.

Not her. Old Randy would never get his hands on Penny. At least not as long as Russ lived and breathed.

"What's his link to Heath?"

"No idea. There's nothing there on Heath."

Joel left a file on Russ's desk. "It's all there."

"Thanks. What about the security video?"

He angled his chin to the folder. "Photos inside. Penny nailed it. A guy in a white shirt and blue baseball cap snuck under the garage gate when someone exited. Looks like your Randy Jones guy. No prints in the apartment. He must have picked the lock. The thing is a piece of junk."

Russ would have to talk to her about changing it. She depended too much on the security outside the building. He flipped the file open. On top sat a rap sheet with a photo of Randy Jones. While chasing the man, Russ hadn't gotten a look at his face. All he'd seen was the back of his head. A head covered with a ball cap that only allowed him to see muddy-brown hair underneath. The hair color looked right. He checked his physical stats. Russ's earlier estimation that the guy had an inch or two on him was about right.

"Okay, Randy Jones, what's your connection to Colin Heath?"

Russ checked the rest of the file, where he found notes on Jones's history and the telltale still photos of him sneaking under the garage gate. *Got him.* Jones was a lifelong Chicago resident. Mostly Evanston—E-Town—population somewhere around eighty thousand and roughly ten miles from downtown Chicago. Also the home of Northwestern University. Colin Heath's alma mater.

Given the prison stints, Russ didn't imagine Jones had gone to Northwestern, but he was only a couple of years younger than Heath. The itch on the back of Russ's neck told him that somehow, Northwestern was the link. Perhaps the two men had a mutual friend that went to the school. Or siblings. Russ jotted a note to compare their families. Could be a connection.

Undoubtedly, Jones was a bad dude and it left a sick feeling in Russ's gut. He checked the time on his desk phone—3:50 p.m. He was scheduled to meet with Elizabeth Brooks for more questioning soon and Penny would be there. He'd fill her in on this development and encourage her to find alternate living arrangements.

Now, though, he wanted to find Randy Jones and see just what the hell he knew about Colin Heath.

It took Russ and his squad mate, Ryan Davis, thirty-nine minutes to navigate traffic on Lake Shore Drive and knock on the door of Jones's apartment. The battered four-story building had definitely seen better days. A television blared from the apartment across the hall and collided with yelling from two people. Man and a woman. Russ blew out a breath, hoping they wouldn't have to intervene on a domestic sitch.

He knocked on Jones's door again and waited. No peephole existed. Russ guessed his suspect would either yell through the door or crack it open. In which case he'd flash his badge and let Randy Jones know he had some explaining to do.

To his surprise, the door flew open and there stood old Randy, still wearing the shorts and white shirt Russ had seen him in earlier and his face a blistering shade of red. "You crazy people!" he hollered.

Russ badged him. "Hello, Randy. Got a minute?"

Immediately, his eyes darted left and right and then to the door across the hall, where the neighbors continued to grapple. Clearly, he'd thought the neighbors had banged on his door and the panic over his mistake quickly stormed his system.

Ryan peered over Jones's shoulder into the apartment and whistled. "I suppose you got a good explanation for that rifle being in your residence. Considering you're on parole."

Nice. Russ angled his head for a look into the small living room. Against the far wall was a blue plaid sofa. Two of the cushions were patched with white material. Strewn across the arm of the sofa was an M24 sniper rifle.

Jones made a move to slam the door and both agents threw their weight against it, forcing their way in. “No chance, pal,” Russ said. “That weapon presents a safety issue and with you being on parole, you’re in violation.”

Russ muscled Jones into the apartment and shoved him against the wall. “Hands against the wall. Let me see ’em. You got anything in your pockets that might hurt me? Needles, anything?”

“I don’t know anything,” Jones said. “The gun isn’t mine.”

“I bet. But that rifle is your ride back to prison. You want to tell us if it was used in that shooting at the courthouse the other day?”

Jones stayed silent. Something was seriously off here. This guy had been in prison for most of his adult life. He couldn’t have been the shooter. Those kinds of shooting skills took hours upon hours of practice. Hours Jones didn’t have because—hey—prisoners generally weren’t allowed to take target practice with sniper rifles.

Now they’d just have to figure out who the weapon belonged to.

AT THE LAKE HOUSE, Penny sat on the sofa across from Elizabeth while they waited for Russell to grace them with his presence. The man was almost two hours late. At least Penny had brought dinner for everyone, a dinner they ate without the tardy FBI agent. And when he showed up he’d better drop to his knees—*as if*—and thank her for prying the extra food away from Brent and the other marshal, who were chowing like men ending a hunger strike.

“You boys,” she hollered to the kitchen, “I’d better not even see you eyeballing the extra plate of food. I’ll know if it’s been tampered with.”

“Relax,” Brent said from his spot at the table. “He’s here anyway.”

A minute later, Russ strode through the back door, his normally neat hair falling over his forehead and his tie loosened. Very un-FBI-like. He carried a file in his hand. "Evening, everyone."

Penny held her hands out. "What? No apology? We've been waiting almost two hours."

He gave her a second of heavy eye contact, then dropped the manila folder he carried onto the coffee table. "Something came up. And I did call."

"What something?"

He turned to Elizabeth. "Randy Jones. You know him?"

Elizabeth stuck out her bottom lip, then slid her head from side to side. "Doesn't sound familiar."

Digging a photo out of the folder, Russ handed it to her. "Recognize him?"

Again, Elizabeth shook her head.

Penny waggled her hand for the photo. "What's this about?"

"This is the guy I was chasing through your neighborhood this morning. He's also the guy who snuck in through your garage gate. You called that one."

A sick feeling made Penny's stomach jump. "I thought you were chasing Heath?"

"So did I. There were two of them. I cut bait on one and went after this guy." He pointed at the photo. "Heath must have been the other one. We're working on any connections they might have to each other."

Penny passed the photo back to Elizabeth and she studied it a moment longer. "I'm sorry. I don't know him."

Russ clucked his tongue. "You sure? His hair might be different now. Longer, shorter, different color."

She looked again and Penny rolled her eyes. "Do you plan on harassing her until she says she knows him?"

Slowly, Russ tilted his head, his facial muscles tensed. And his eyes. Slightly narrowed and glaring. The look could have melted stone.

Penny held up a hand. "I'm sorry. That was out of line. But she said she doesn't know him."

Russ set the photo on the coffee table in front of Elizabeth. "Think about it. For now, we'll move on."

Except, Penny wasn't ready to move on. She wanted to know what Randy Jones had been doing spying on her that afternoon. Worse, if they'd tracked him down that fast, he must have a record, and having a convicted felon following her didn't offer comfort.

She stood, smacked Russ on the side of his arm. "I need a word. Elizabeth, we'll be right back."

He followed her into the kitchen, where Brent had made himself scarce. Probably outside watching the perimeter with the other marshal. Penny shut the kitchen door, spun and folded her arms. "Spill it, Russell."

He wore the expression she'd seen in her apartment earlier. The sucking-his-cheeks-in one. His thinking face. "And no holding out. I agreed to your terms this afternoon. Now I expect you to be honest with me. The man in that photo broke into my home and he must have a criminal record if you found him already"

Russ leaned back on the granite countertop, folded his arms and met her gaze. "He's in the system."

"I'm assuming from the photo of him entering my garage, you think this was the person who flooded my bathroom. He was in my home and then he stood across the street—with Colin Heath no less—and waited for the excitement to begin. I've seen this in other cases. Heck, I've hired profilers to tell me about post-offense behavior. I should be used to it. And yet, I'm appalled. Go figure."

Russ dropped his arms, blew out a breath. "But now it's personal. Unfortunately, it's not uncommon. Some unsubs taunt the media, send investigators notes, anything to inject themselves into the process. Could be what he's doing."

"Does he have a history of this type of behavior?"

"He's been in prison twice. Robbery and aggravated kidnapping." Penny opened her mouth, but he held up his hand. "Let me finish."

She closed her mouth.

"Thank you." He gave her a half smile. "You're getting good at listening to me."

"Don't push me, Russell."

"He's out on parole. We tracked him down at his apartment."

She moved to where he stood and leaned against the counter. This close she could see the dark circles marring the underside of his eyes. Exhaustion had obviously closed in. And here he was, doing his job, questioning his witness so he could close this case. Some would have gone home and crawled into their bed.

Not Russ.

Big. Trouble. Every excuse she had for not having a man in her life—they didn't understand her work ethic and her long hours—was slowly being dismantled by the sexy FBI agent.

She couldn't think about that now. *Later.* "He just let you in?"

"Hell no. He thought we were the crazy couple across the hall. They were screaming at each other and he opened the door thinking it was the wife. I guess they fight a lot and she bangs on his door. What she wants a convicted felon to do, who knows?"

"A real Boy Scout, huh?"

"Not nearly, babe. Anyway, in the apartment, we found a sniper rifle."

"Ha! Parole violation. He's gone."

Russ grinned at her. "We locked him up while we run ballistics on the rifle. Might be the one used in the courthouse shooting. He's not talking, though."

Now she was confused. The man had spent years in prison. Where'd he learn sharpshooting skills? "Is he a sniper?"

Russ scoffed, "With his record? When would he have time?"

"That's what I thought."

He glanced at the plate of food she'd set aside for him. He had to be starving. Unless he'd hit the drive-through. "Are you hungry? I wrestled food from Brent. And when I say 'wrestled,' I mean it. That man can eat."

"You saved me dinner?"

She batted her eyes. "Yes. Despite the fact that you were late. If you're hungry, I'll warm it up while you start with Elizabeth."

For a second he stood there, eyebrows slightly raised, perhaps a little stunned. Which, in truth, she wasn't sure if she should be hurt by. Did he think so little of her that she wouldn't save him a meal?

"You're surprised I saved you dinner."

"No. You're giving that way. I'm surprised that, with what you've been through, you thought of it. You'd have every excuse not to have remembered and you did it anyway. You're a helluva woman, Penny Hennings."

Now, that was an answer she liked. Criminal how good this man was. *Criminal.* "You should drop to your knees and thank me."

That cracked him up and it was an honest-to-goodness curl-a-girl's-toes laugh. *I'm so crushing on him.* Penny watched him, took in the laugh lines around his eyes and imagined him thirty years from now, those same dark eyes, those same laugh lines, only deeper. He'd be one of those annoying men who'd get better-looking with age. As impossible as it seemed, because—heck—he was darned good-looking now.

When he caught her staring, he took her up on it and stared right back and—hello, Mr. Sexy FBI Agent—the heat in an otherwise air-conditioned room spiked. Had Elizabeth not been in the next room, my, oh, my, Penny would have pounced on Russ Voight with the abandon of a woman in desperate need of attention.

"Anyway," he said, "Jones has an older brother who's former military. Got out three years ago. We're running it down. If he was a sniper, the rifle is probably his. And if that rifle was used in the shooting, Randy Jones won't want to be charged with murder."

"His third strike. That's twenty-five to life."

"Yep. If the rifle is a match, I'll flip him. Get him to give us the shooter and Heath."

A solid plan. One Penny would give her favorite stilettos to watch. She imagined Russ in an interview room, his suit jacket unbuttoned, arms crossed, but casually leaning back. His body language would purposely be all over the place. He'd want the emotional firepower to put his suspect on edge as he told him he was sunk. *So hot.*

Penny ignored the twinge in her lower belly, shoved the plate into the microwave and hit a few buttons. "What's his connection to Heath?"

"Don't know yet. Heath grew up in a cushy upscale suburb and went to Northwestern. Jones lived in Evanston on and off, so that might be the connection. Heath and the brother are about the same age. I'm running that down, too. I should know more in a couple of hours. Right now, I need to talk with Elizabeth. The more we have from her, combined with any possible developments from today, will only get us closer to Heath."

"Well, *Russell,* let's get back to work, then. Head in there and I'll bring your food when it's ready."

At least then she wouldn't be tempted to strip her clothes off.

RUSS STUDIED HIS NOTES before going back to Elizabeth. Three hours they'd been at it and his brain had lost its snap long ago. A slouching Elizabeth, her eye makeup smudged and dragging down her cheeks, didn't exactly look energized, either. "We're almost done for the night."

"I'm okay," she said. "I'd rather get it over with."

Penny leaned over and nudged her with her shoulder. "You're doing great. This has to be difficult."

"Yes and no. It's almost a relief. I want this man out of our lives. He took my son's father away. If I don't help convict Heath, he'll torment me for the rest of my life. He's crazy that way. Once he gets his hooks in, he doesn't let go."

"Did you know your husband threatened to turn him in?" Russ asked.

"No. At that point, I didn't even know he was doing anything illegal."

He eyed her. Whether she truly believed that, he couldn't tell. Unconsciously, she could have convinced herself.

"I knew he was stressed and I questioned him. Maybe I was suspicious of his behavior but I wasn't sure what I was suspicious of. I didn't think he'd break laws. Then, when he was killed, I wasn't sure of anything. At least until Heath contacted me and told me what they were doing and that Sam had taken money from him. I didn't know anything about that. I swear to you. I went along to save my son. I made the trades and I've saved copies of everything. I knew I wouldn't be able to stomach Heath's dirty work for long, but I needed time to figure out what to do. Working for Heath got me that time. Keeping my son safe was the only option."

Russ jotted more notes. Some of this she'd already told him, but he'd record it all, check for inconsistencies later. "What about the safe-deposit boxes?"

"I found the keys and opened all the boxes where the money was. I assumed it was Heath's and took it to him. He was happy to relieve me of it, but wouldn't let me out of the scam."

"That's when you went to Penny?"

"Yes. I'd actually thought if I returned the money, he'd let me go. I'm stupid."

"You're not stupid," Penny interjected. "I don't want to hear that from you."

"She's right," Russ said.

Penny swung to him with a look of wide-eyed shock. What? She couldn't believe he'd be supportive? He scratched the back of his neck and dug in until his nails bit skin. The temporary pain distracted him from other things he felt. One being the hurt that came with a woman he'd been lusting after for months, and had grown to care about, thinking he was heartless.

Back to work. "You said you saved copies of everything. Where are those copies?"

"I put them in the safe-deposit boxes where the money was."

Elizabeth rose from her spot and walked to the closet near the staircase. Penny glanced at Russ and shrugged. Elizabeth returned with a purse that could double as an overnight bag. What the hell did women carry in those things that they needed them available at all times? She set the bag on the table and dug through it until she unearthed a quart-size Baggie.

"Here are the box keys. I took them with me when you brought us here. I should have turned them over earlier. I'm sorry. I was… I guess I was scared."

Russ stayed quiet for a second, mesmerized by the bag in Elizabeth's hand. There they were. Literally the keys to evidence that might finally break open his case. Twelve months of work and it culminated in a quart-size sandwich bag. His body turned rigid, his head slamming—*bam, bam, bam*—as he breathed in, attempted to control his emotions, because, finally, he'd get this guy.

He reached for the bag, but Elizabeth inched back. "This is everything I have. The only copies."

Penny scooted next to Elizabeth and slid one arm around her. "It's okay. He'll take care of it. I promise you."

If Elizabeth needed convincing, he'd convince her. Maybe not in the soft way Penny chose to, because, if it came down to it, his way involved the threat of a prison sentence. He didn't want to go there, though. Not if he didn't have to.

Penny held her palm flat in front of her. "It's okay."

Elizabeth stared down at Penny's hand, gripped the Baggie tighter, then turned to him. "This is my son's life in this bag."

Russ sat forward, looked her dead-on. "Of all your options, I'm the best one. The FBI can give you a new life somewhere. For me to make that happen, I need those keys."

His head continued to pound, but he waited. He'd learned silence could sometimes be an asset. Typically, the one who spoke first lost. Right now, he hoped there'd be no losers, but he'd damn sure not be the first to speak.

Elizabeth dropped the bag in Penny's hand. Russ stared at it a second, forcing himself to not react, to keep his body language in check. To stay neutral. He inhaled, let the burst of oxygen settle his mind. The pounding in his head eased and he exhaled, took a second to get his thoughts in order.

"It's all yours," she said.

"Thank you."

Only, Penny curled her fingers around the bag and Russ slid his gaze to her. *What's this, now?*

"I go with you to the banks. I want to document everything she turns over."

Easily, he could tell her to go scratch, but she was Elizabeth's lawyer. If anything, she'd insist on seeing the evidence first.

"I'm throwing you a bone here, Russell. I could go through all this evidence before you even get a peek at it."

"It's a lot," Elizabeth said.

A slow, smug—*damn, that's smoking*—grin slid across

Penny's face. "I'm sure it is. It could take me a month to go through it all."

Killer Cupcake. She may have been tough, but he wasn't afraid of her. Not much anyway. And really, he didn't care if she went with him. They'd have to do some evasive maneuvering to get them both into the banks at the same time, since Heath was watching her, but they'd pull it off. They'd been managing to get her to the safe house without being tailed, so sneaking into a city bank with pedestrian traffic shouldn't be an issue.

He flopped out his hand. "Agreed. Hand over those keys."

She snatched her hand back and walked to the kitchen. A minute later she returned with Brent.

"You're my witness," she said to him.

Now, this was priceless. "Please. He's a government agent. You can't use him."

"He's here and I'm using him. It'll keep you honest." She turned to Brent. "Elizabeth is about to turn over keys to—" she stopped, counted the keys in the bag "—four safe-deposit boxes. Agent Voight has just agreed to let me accompany him to retrieve and document the evidence contained in said boxes. You're my witness that he agreed to this."

Brent pointed at Russ. "Did you agree to that?"

"I did."

"Fine. I'm a witness. Am I done?"

Penny nodded. "Yes. Thank you."

Russ held his hand out again. "Let's have 'em."

He watched her. Waited to see if she'd come up with more stipulations. Wouldn't shock him if she did. The woman was a shark. If he didn't play this right, she'd devour him. Rip off his limbs and leave him a bloody stump. Both professionally and personally.

And he loved it.

Chapter Eleven

Colin Heath stood in front of the Criminal Court Building, the bright morning sun heating up the pavement as the temperature climbed to almost ninety. In May. By noon they'd be close to a hundred.

Yeah. Turning up the heat.

He sipped his iced latte—too heavy on the milk—and leaned back against the light pole. Heat from the scorching pole plunged through his T-shirt, reminding him to stay focused. Second time this week he'd been at this building, watching the action. Perhaps he should have stayed away today, given the heightened security, but something inside wouldn't allow it. He needed to see it. Feel the pleasure of stripping all power and control from that Hennings bitch.

Stupid woman.

He shifted an inch to a more comfortable spot and searing heat stabbed at him.

Soon.

A young blonde cruised toward him wearing cutoffs and a tank top, and he tipped his glasses low, gave her a look that said he'd absolutely noticed her. Here he was, a harmless guy in cargo shorts and a T-shirt, waiting on a friend. Too bad the blonde couldn't be that friend. Even if she probably wasn't legal drinking age, he didn't need her for drinking. He'd think of better things to do with that body.

Although the silly office assistant from Hennings & Solomon had been keeping him satisfied. Still, her usefulness was waning. Considering she thought he was an advertising salesman named Joe, there was only so much information he could pry from her regarding her employers. Poor, naive young woman. Too bad.

The blonde averted her gaze. A shame. He could have had fun with her. *Next time.*

His phone rang and he slid it from his pocket as the blonde's exceptional rear left his sight. "What's up?"

"He's coming out."

Ah, yes. The mission. "Thank you. You ready?"

"Yeah. I'm heading down now. Van is ready."

The plan was simple. Almost too simple, but Colin excelled at the success of exceptionally simple plans. For years now he'd been bilking investors out of their money, creating a way of life for himself most would only dream of, a taste of triumph that left him hungry for more. And if people were willing to turn over their pensions, well, he couldn't help that. He had a business to run.

Colin clicked off, stared casually down the street—*I'm a harmless guy waiting on a friend*—and spotted his target coming down the courthouse steps. *Ding. Ding. Ding.*

At six foot three, Zac Hennings was easy to spot. Now they needed timing to be their friend because the U.S. marshal beside Hennings wouldn't make this easy. Two light poles down, a maintenance worker in coveralls dumped a tool bag.

Hennings strode toward him, head high. Sure, he'd varied his pattern in terms of his morning routine, but some things couldn't be changed. He no longer stopped at Starbucks first thing, but he had to do his job. And doing his job meant trips to the courthouse. For Heath, it had been easy. He parked himself at the courthouse and when Zac went in, Heath put his plan in motion while waiting for his target to exit.

Easy. Pickings.

The U.S. marshal walked beside Hennings, appearing unruffled but observant, casually checking their surroundings.

Heath glanced up to the maintenance worker, who made eye contact. All was well. Hennings walked by him as a white cargo van lumbered down the block. Timing. Timing. Timing.

Colin reached up, adjusted the bill of his baseball cap and stepped sideways as the maintenance worker spun, caught the marshal off guard and jabbed a needle into his shoulder. The aim should have been for the neck and all that vulnerable vascularization, but the shoulder would do. Even if it took a minute longer for the drug to take effect.

"Ho!" Zac yelled as the maintenance worker fled across the street into a waiting car. Heath sipped his latte, stared straight ahead as a woman stopped to render aid. *No need, my love.* Another pedestrian—teenager—skirted around the threesome, his head swinging back and forth, clearly unsure. *Go about your business.*

Still, Heath remained in his spot. Watching. Waiting.

"Run," the marshal yelled, lurching forward and dropping to the ground as the medication took hold.

A shrill scream came from the woman and Hennings bent low to check his marshal. Oh, yes. So easy.

The van pulled into the fire zone—about time—and the side door slid open with a bang. Heath boosted off the light pole. Two men in ski masks leaped out and Hennings rose from his crouched position. The two men snagged him by both arms and he kicked out, landing a shot at one of his attacker's knees.

Warm blood rushed through Heath's veins and he breathed in. Enjoyed the stir of emotions. The erection finally came and he wanted the blonde back. Somehow, watching the action, knowing he controlled it, did that to him. Aroused him.

At the van, Zac continued his battle. Two civilians ran for him, pounced on the attackers. At least until the barrel of the rifle was presented to them.

The bystanders jumped away—*yes, gentlemen, be smart*—and Zac disappeared into the van's gaping door.

Sirens sounded in the distance. Too late. The van pulled away, merging into traffic.

Heath glanced at the marshal on the ground, then back to the fleeing van. Simple plans. Always the best kind.

RUSS SAT IN HIS CUBICLE, preparing for his impending conversation with Randy Jones, who would soon have a decision to make because the rifle found in his possession matched slugs taken from the courthouse incident. An incident that left an innocent woman dead.

In short, Randy Jones was cooked and all he had to do to get out of it was tell Russ who'd fired that weapon. Russ's desk phone bleeped. He glanced across the stacks of folders and memos cluttering the desktop—other active cases being ignored—then focused on the phone. The thing had rung three times but each time he'd let it go to voice mail rather than interrupt his momentum. The bleeping, as opposed to ringing, was the receptionist using the intercom. Someone was looking for him in a bad way.

He grabbed the handset. "I'm here. Sorry. I was in the middle of something."

"I have Brent Thompson for you."

Brent. Calling him. What was this, now? "Put him through. Thanks."

He disconnected the intercom and waited five beats for the line to ring. "What's up, Brent?"

On the other end of the phone line, voices carried, a door slammed, followed by silence in the background. Brent must have moved into an office and closed the door. *Privacy.* Which couldn't be good news. An immediate zap shot to Russ's brain. He tapped his fingers against the handset. *Wait for it.*

"Straight out," Brent said. "Someone snatched Zac Hennings."

Three things registered: one, Zac Hennings had been kidnapped; two, how the hell did that happen; and three, where was the U.S. marshal supposedly protecting him?

Russ stood, took one step, then realized he was anchored to the desk by the phone cord. Nowhere to go. He peeked over the metal cubicle wall to Ryan's workspace on the other side. If he were there, he could start making calls, trying to figure out what the hell happened to Zac Hennings.

No Ryan.

Two agents huddled together a few desks down, but otherwise, no one could be seen above the rows of identical cubicle walls. He went back to Brent. "What the hell happened?"

"He was coming out of the courthouse."

Russ made a fist and swung into dead air. *Damn it.* There was only so much he could do to protect the Hennings family. Penny had remarked her brother liked routine. A routine Russ had warned him to vary.

"Before you go off," Brent said, "he's been changing his patterns. The guy has to do his job and they caught him coming out of a hearing. Heath must have been waiting for him."

The ASAC's office sat in a line of glass-walled offices along the outer ring of the building and Russ craned his neck to get his attention. Couldn't see. Too far down. "Where's Zac's marshal?"

"At the hospital. Unsubs loaded him up on some kind of tranquilizer. Local P.D. responded, informed my boss and it took them an hour to call me."

"He's been gone an hour?"

"As soon as I heard, I called you."

"Where are you?"

"In a conference room near Penny's office."

She'd go over the edge when she heard this. "And she's where?"

"In her office. If I have to tie her down, she's not leaving this suite. She doesn't know yet. The higher-ups from both our offices are talking as we speak. I figured I'd check in with you."

On the far end of the office, Ryan strode from the men's room. The men's room. Nature simply wasn't Russ's friend. Whatever. He held his free hand up, waved Ryan over and went back to Brent. "Get Penny away from the phone and television until I get there. Lock her in that boardroom if necessary but do not let her take any calls. She'll throw a damned fit, but you're a smart guy—figure it out. My guess is Heath will contact her. If I know this guy at all, he'll want to tell her about Zac. Let's beat him to it. Take away his edge."

"I'm on it."

From the other end of the phone, a muffled shriek sounded. Russ's body buzzed—arms, legs, torso—all of it heating up as the wailing from Brent's end became louder.

"Too late," Brent said. "I think she knows."

Chapter Twelve

Russ slammed the phone back in its cradle, grabbed his suit jacket off his chair, snatched up his cell phone and started for the elevator. Ryan came at him, holding up his hands. "You got that shoot-me look. What's up?"

Russ kept moving, speaking as he passed his coworker. "Can't stop. I'm about to call you on your cell. Pick up."

Along the way, he scrolled his contacts, found Ryan's number and as he passed the receptionist told her he'd be at Hennings & Solomon.

He pressed the elevator button, saw it light up on the ground floor. *Get there.* No time to wait. He hit the stairwell and hauled tail down the steps. Penny's office was six blocks south. Between traffic and stoplights, he'd spend twenty minutes trying to get there by car, or he could hoof it, in the stifling heat that would give him a stroke, and get there in five. But he'd be without wheels.

Twenty versus five. *She needs help.* He had to get there. *She might be next.* Pounding down the steps, he concentrated on containing the situation. *Brent's on her.* Whether his emotions were purely about Zac or needing to be close to Penny, he didn't know. All he knew, without a doubt, was he had to get to her.

Looked as if he was hoofing it.

Minutes later, he stormed into Hennings & Solomon,

sweat pouring from his face onto his already soaked-through shirt, and, yeah, he probably smelled ripe.

The receptionist rolled her lips back and angled away. He'd just sprinted through unbearable heat—what did she expect? "Penny and Brent. Where?"

He wouldn't get charm-school points for that greeting, but it got her moving.

She pointed to the door. "They just left."

"What?"

Had he heard that right? Maybe the heat fried his brain? He'd told Brent to sit tight. Wait. *Had* he? *Don't know.* From his pocket, his cell phone rang and he dug it out. Brent.

"Where are you?"

"On our way to Penny's. Total cluster. Heath told her she had fifteen minutes to get there or Zac..."

Brent cleared his throat, obviously not wanting to finish the statement in front of Penny.

"I get it. Why her apartment?"

"Said he'd call the landline with further instructions."

Trap. Russ paced the reception area, dragged his free hand through his damp hair. "Could be a setup."

"Yep."

"You got backup for when you get there?"

"They're on the way. We'll clear the apartment before she goes in."

Good man. "I'll take care of the phones. See if we can get a trace." Russ wrapped the thumb and third finger of his free hand around his forehead and squeezed. Crazy pressure. "How is she?"

"Not good."

Russ stopped walking, let the words sink in. Adrenaline made his head throb and he squeezed his forehead harder. Penny needed help and he couldn't seem to get to her. "Let me talk to her."

"Hang on."

A long minute passed and Penny finally came on. "Russell?"

And, oh, damn, her voice. Broken. *Shredded.* The gravelly sound of a postcrying jag. Penny in tears. All of it so un–Killer Cupcake. Russ hustled out of the office, headed for the emergency steps and stopped before he lost the call—and her—in the stairwell.

"Hi, honey. I'm on this. The marshal's office and my office are already working it. We have people en route to the scene now. We'll find Zac. I promise you."

Even if he's dead. He shouldn't let his mind go there. He knew it, but he'd been at this job long enough to know how this could play out. Zac Hennings might already be gone.

"Okay," she said.

Okay? No screaming, no hollering, no drama. Bad news all around. But through a phone line, there wasn't much he could do. "I'm on my way to your place. Where's your father?"

"He's at a meeting across town. He doesn't know. I have to tell him." She paused and he heard the sharp intake of breath. "How am I supposed to tell him?"

"We'll figure it out. Just get home."

"I hate this man. I *hate* him. I want him dead."

The only bright spot was the return of Killer Cupcake. That was who they needed now and they needed her at her fighting best. "I know."

"I want to squeeze his neck in my hands and watch the life drain from him. He stole my brother."

PENNY STOOD IN THE MIDDLE of her living room, in her secure building where no harm would come to her, and knew it was all a lie. Her supposed sanctuary was a joke.

Zac's gone. Waiting for that stupid call, the cordless phone she held grew slick. She squeezed it, sending every ounce of anger and hurt and pressure into her fingers. Starting at her knees, an involuntary quaking grew, then slithered up her thighs, into her hips, over her torso until finally, the insanity of it all, the horror of her brother being kidnapped—possibly murdered—crashed inside her.

Get it together. Don't cry, don't cry, don't cry.

She squeezed the phone tighter, moved to the window, turned and came back. At any second, Heath would be calling. Or maybe he wouldn't. Maybe getting her here was a game. A way to control her. She wouldn't put it past the sick, degenerate animal.

The phone rang.

She stared at it for half a second while the harsh *bling-bling-bling* clawed against her nerves, punishing her already battered brain. *This is it.*

She needed Russ. If nothing else, just for his presence. Brent was in the hall, where she'd made him wait because she needed a minute alone. He'd objected, of course, obviously fearing she'd harm herself, but one thing about her, she knew how to persuade men to do things they didn't agree with.

Besides, he didn't give her the sense of calm Russ did. Russ had a way of communicating with her, of making her feel safe without weakening her. Brent didn't have that. Maybe it was his hugeness or the way he sometimes came off as pushy, unyielding. She didn't know. All she knew was Russ didn't make her feel that way.

Russ also wouldn't have left her alone.

But Russ wasn't here and the phone had just rung for the third time. She hit the button. "Hello?"

"Lovely Penny."

Sick, demented monster.

She breathed in, visualized her hands around this man's neck and squeezing. She'd only ever seen him in photos, but it was enough where she had an image in her mind. "Save it, Heath. Put my brother on."

"In good time, my dear. He is, in fact, on the way to this location."

Long drive. Where was he taking him?

"Then why am I here? Aside from you taking pleasure in ordering me around."

Heath laughed, but it was one of those fake, salesmen laughs. "How well you know me."

"You're fairly predictable."

Fast comeback aside, she bit her bottom lip. The man had stolen her brother—maybe now might be the time to show a bit of fear.

Even with her love for her brother, she wasn't sure how to do that. How to become a weak female incapable of handling a life-shattering event.

Besides, Zac would hate that.

"Maybe so," Heath said. "But if you'd like your brother to remain alive, you will turn the widow over to me. Or better yet, tell me where I can find her. She's still talking and I'm done waiting. Do not move from your apartment or your brother is dead. Do not call the FBI. Do *not* call the attentive Special Agent Voight. I'm watching and I'll kill them all. I'll call you back on this line with instructions."

Silence followed. A burst of dead air that made Penny's pulse kick.

"Hello?" She pulled the phone down, stared at the screen a second—for what reason she had no idea—and put it to her ear again. "Heath?"

Her only link to Zac and he'd hung up. She squeezed the phone, let the twinge of pressure slide through her fingers into her wrist. *Stay calm.*

If ever there was a time she should be allowed to throw a fit, it should be now. Her brother was gone.

And it was her fault.

Fear curled into her throat, choking her, making her gasp at its ferocity. How had a financial-fraud case spun so far from her control?

She threw the phone. Just slammed that sucker against the wall and watched it shatter into three pieces. The only sound in her apartment was the churn of the air conditioning, that low hum that often relaxed her, but now? Now it reminded her how alone she was.

A knock sounded on her apartment door. *Brent.* "You okay in there?"

Get it together. If she didn't, he'd be busting in here and she didn't want him to see her in full meltdown mode. She didn't want anyone to see her this way. So much for the fearless defense attorney.

"I'm fine," she called. "Having a little hissy fit. Occasionally, I do that."

Right. Make him think this was normal behavior. Why not?

From the coffee table, her cell phone rang and the dual vibration caused a rumbling sound.

She dived for it. Checked the number. "Russell?" Her voice cracked and—*I'm losing it*—tears filled her eyes. She shoved her thumb and middle finger against her closed eyes, praying the tears would stop. Tears, she didn't need. She drew a breath, let it out. *I shouldn't talk to him.* "You can't come here."

"I'm two blocks away. Traffic is nuts and I had to wait for a cab because I ran to your office."

Two blocks. *He'll be here soon.* "You *ran* to my office?"

"Faster that way. Probably not the smartest move, but at the time it seemed like a good option."

"Heath called. Just now. Don't come here."

"Stop talking to me and write everything down. Right now. Before you forget."

She nodded. Some defense attorney. That should have been the first thing she'd done. *You know better.* "He said no FBI. Please. He's calling me back and he's watching."

"Penny, I promise you, he won't see me."

Russ swung out of the elevator on Penny's floor and halted. Brent stood, hands on hips, squared off with Penny's closed apartment door. What she'd done this time, Russ didn't know, but Brent's stiff body language transmitted one seriously pissed-off dude.

He swung his head in Russ's direction. Yep. Pissed. "What'd she do?"

"She won't open it. I've been talking to the door for five minutes. How am I supposed to help her if she locks me out? I'm about to kick in this damned door."

Time to chill. Russ stepped closer and, as he'd hoped, Brent backed away. One thing he'd noticed about Brent, he didn't like people in his space. "She got the call," Russ said.

The enormous marshal threw his hands up. "That explains it. I heard a crash, but she said she was having a hissy fit and was fine. Since then, nothing. Total darkness. I knew I shouldn't have left her alone."

She's far from fine. "She can be convincing." Russ angled between Brent and the door and knocked. "It's Russ. Open up."

Three seconds later, the door flew open.

Penny stood in the doorway, her suit jacket off and a thin, silky tank top clinging to her torso. Russ refused to acknowledge the outline of her bra cups through the white shirt. *Not going there.*

He glanced back at Brent, who was just as red-blooded as Russ and had definitely acknowledged the cups. *Time to break this up.* Russ slid into the doorway and nudged Penny inside before turning back. "I got Penny. Do me a favor and head back to your office. See what you can shake loose."

"You sure?"

"Yeah. We're good here."

He closed the door and faced Penny. Maybe later he'd mention she shouldn't open the door dressed like a fantasy from a lingerie catalog when two single men stood on the other side.

Back to business here.

Except, Penny stood there, six inches away, gazing up at him with huge blue eyes that had been sucked of all their sparking energy. Killer Cupcake, slaughtered.

"You okay?"

She reached out, curled her fingers into his shirt and squeezed. Her knuckles pushed through the shirt to skin and he glanced down. Before he had a chance to look back at her, she rested her head against his chest. "I don't know what to do."

"Ah, Penny. I'm sorry."

"He's gone, Russell."

He rubbed his palms over her arms—her freezing arms—and squeezed. "We'll find him. I promise you. We'll find him. There's nowhere Heath can hide. We're talking to everyone he knows. I got ballistics back on the rifle and it's a match. Someone is working on Randy Jones now. Soon we'll have the shooter and he'll tell us where Heath is. We'll make it happen."

Finally, she glanced up, met his gaze briefly and then focused on his mouth.

And, if Russ knew women, which he was fairly sure he did, Penny was about to kiss the hell out of him.

And he wouldn't fight it, which was a problem.

"Did anyone see you enter the building?" she asked.

"No. I called your doorman. Cab dropped me a block away and I weaved through the alleys. The doorman let me in the service entrance in the back alley."

"You're sure?"

"I'm sure."

Again her gaze went to his mouth.

"Penny, you're fine."

"No, I'm not. I'm a total screwup."

And then she did it. She gripped his shirt harder, slid

to her toes and kissed him. Long and slow and soft. *I'm toast.* From somewhere inside—he'd never know where—he found the good sense to break the kiss.

"This isn't what you need."

"Actually, it is."

Um, okay.

"And I don't want to think too hard about it, because that's where we'll mess it up. My brother is gone and there's nothing I can do but sit here, useless, waiting for the next call. That's all I can do."

"Listen to me—"

"I don't want to listen. I want to fight. For my brother. I brought this to my family and I can't fix it. The guilt and anger and hurt are killing me and I hate myself—*hate,* Russell—and I have to tell my parents. My dad has been locked in an off-site client meeting all morning and I'm not telling my mother until my dad can be with her. At this moment, there is nothing I can do to fix this. It's my fault and I need someone—you—to remind me I'm good at something. To tell me I'm not a failure. You and I, together, will not be a failure. I know it."

Huh. This was a first. On many levels. The first being Killer Cupcake having a meltdown. The second being a defense attorney throwing herself at him. And him liking it.

She slid her arms around him and—yep, she was going to lay another one on him. He sucked in a breath and waited for that second when her lips would hit his and his body would ignite all over again.

Bam. She kissed him. *Hang on, hang on, hang on.* He hesitated. At least until she crushed herself against him, wanting him to pick up the pace. Control. That was what he needed here.

What *she* needed now wasn't fast, hard sex. She needed slow and quiet. Yep. That was what she needed. Whether she knew it or not.

Maybe he'd give her both. He squeezed her arms and broke the kiss.

She stepped back. "What's the problem?"

Where should he start? He had a list.

"First, I have a technical agent on the way here to rig your phone. Second, we're not rushing through this. You're all keyed up, and that's probably a crummy reason for us to go back on our agreement to steer clear of a physical relationship."

The lines between her brows deepened. "Russell Voight, sometimes I want to hate you, but most times I'm just thankful."

"For what?"

"For you. As crazy as you make me, I love when you're around."

Well, damn. Not what he'd expected. He stepped forward, grabbed her hand and, one by one, skimmed her fingers, working the tension from them as he went. When he'd flattened the last finger, he dipped his head, kissed her palm. *Don't do this.*

Her sharp inhalation shattered his concentration and he glanced up in time for her to ease forward and wrap her arms around his waist. He ran his hand over her head, twirled the long blond strands over his fingers, and her shoulders shook. Crying.

"Oh, baby, I'm sorry."

"My parents will never forgive me. I'll never forgive me."

She squeezed him tighter and deep sobs ripped into her. Killer Cupcake unglued. But she looked up at him, those lush lips right there, and jerk that he was, he knew what he wanted. What they both wanted.

He did the only thing he could. He bent low, scooped her up and headed to her bedroom. Her face transformed into wide-eyed shock that beat the hell out of seeing her in tears. "You're all mine."

She wiggled around, smacked him on the chest. "Russell!"

There we go.

"Russell! You are *not* manhandling me in my own home."

"Yeah, I am. You need it." He grinned. "You need a lot of things. And I plan on giving them to you."

She kicked her legs and almost blasted him in the crotch. "Hey, now. Don't damage the equipment before you've used it."

She gasped. "Pig!"

Damn, he loved rattling her. Making her forget the nightmare currently known as her life.

Once in her bedroom he tossed—yep, tossed—her on the bed and waited half a second for the yelling. *One, two, three.*

No yelling.

"You're quiet," he said, slipping off his tie and unbuttoning his collar.

More than a little heavy on the eye contact, she sat up and tore the cami over her head and Russ stood, like some fumbling high schooler, paralyzed by the sight of her. *Do something, man.* For months he'd been fantasizing about Penny Hennings naked and now all he wanted was to slow her down. Let him savor each piece of clothing coming off so he could seal it into his subconscious.

He set one knee on the bed and grabbed her hands. "Go slower for me, okay?"

A sexy grin quirked one side of her mouth, a look he'd seen on her before and recognized. The look of assuming control. Yes, he'd just given Killer Cupcake all the power. She'd eat him alive.

"Russell?"

"Yeah?"

"I'm thinking about all the things I want you to do to me."

Well, hell. He threw his head back, tried not to think about his raging erection straining against his pants and her hands at the button of his waistband.

"Still want me to go slow?" she cracked.

And, if for no other reason than to drive her—and maybe

himself—insane, he stepped back. "I do. I've been thinking about this a long time. I want it to last."

Still on the bed, she got to her knees, gripped his shirt and kissed him. Slow and gentle, just as he'd said he wanted, and something in his brain fired. Pent-up frustration—*need*—tore into him. She'd mess him up in a million different ways. His career, his emotions, all of it would be hers.

And he didn't mind.

For once with her it wouldn't be about control or winning or losing. For once, they'd both get what they wanted.

He reached around and unhooked her bra, slid the straps down her shoulders, and she backed away, letting him see her. Just as he'd asked. Killer Cupcake giving him what he wanted.

"You're beautiful. Maybe a little mouthy, but I like mouthy women."

That teasing smile quirked again. "Russell, shut up and kiss me."

Damn. Could be love.

Kiss her he did. Long and slow while he explored every inch of her, living out his fantasy of soft skin under his fingers. He unzipped her skirt and slid it down. *Slow, slow, slow.* She lowered herself to the bed and let him take the skirt the rest of the way off, his fingers moving down the soft curve of her thigh. Dang, she was tiny.

Delicate.

Something he'd never imagined from Killer Cupcake.

And then he gave up on slow and was on top of her, devouring her. Lips, cheeks, neck, breasts, all of it, there for him to feast on after all these months. She dug her fingers into his hair, gripped hard, and an inferno whipped at his skin.

He wanted her.

Now.

Chapter Thirteen

Penny inhaled a hard breath while Russ's mouth magically reached all the places she'd imagined. Finally. They'd fought it long enough. *You're using him.* She opened her eyes, stared at the ceiling. No. Not using him. Needing him. Needing him to distract her from her failures. To love her.

She slammed her eyes closed again, willed her brain to stop. *Please.* Just a couple of minutes of peace. That was all she wanted.

In a flurry, she pushed Russ away, rolled him to his back and straddled him. Too many clothes. With fast but fumbling fingers, she unbuttoned his shirt only to find a T-shirt.

"Russell, you're such a pain. Get rid of these shirts."

He laughed, then sat up, but held her with one hand so she didn't go anywhere. She pushed the dress shirt off his shoulders and pulled his T-shirt off. Underneath, just as she'd pictured, was all hard muscle and cut angles. She kissed his bare shoulder and he groaned.

"I love how you feel," she said.

He tossed her off. "I've got to get these pants off."

"Yes, you do." She stretched out on her bed, keeping her gaze on his and grinning like a fool. Why not? She rather enjoyed this playful side. She didn't allow it to happen often, but Russ brought it out in her and she'd be forever grateful for that. She patted the spot next to her. "Come and get me."

"Pffft."

Penny cracked up, but the size of his erection silenced her. "Wow."

"Now who's laughing?"

Never one to shy away from a challenge, she hooked one foot around his leg. "I'm waiting."

She didn't need to wait long. Well, maybe the condom took a minute longer than she appreciated, but, well, safe sex and all that. Finally, he hovered over her, propped on his elbows, his fingers gently moving over her face and into her hair.

So tender. Something she'd never imagined between them. She glided one leg along his, their bodies so perfectly aligned—melded—and the skin-to-skin friction shot into her lower belly, the heat settling there, making her want more. Of what, she wasn't sure. Sex. Him. Both.

Yes, both. She wrapped her hand around the back of his head. "We'll go slower next time."

If he'd planned on arguing, he'd abandoned it when she wrapped her legs around his hips, waiting, anticipating that amazing first moment when he would enter her. Slowly, he shifted and she brought her legs higher and—*yes*—he inched his way, bit by little bit, and she gasped.

A low groan came from Russ and she pumped her hips, letting Mr. Go Slow know he'd better pick up the pace. Ooh, she wanted to kill him. Just smack him one for torturing her. But that slow slide, the feel of this man inside her, sent shivers along her skin.

Finally. A man she could love. A man who accepted her zany, pushy personality. And liked her anyway.

"It's so perfect," she said.

He smiled down at her, kissed her, and she held on, wanting only more. More. More. More. Forever.

He shifted again and her body seized. She closed her eyes, breathed in and waited.

She rocked her hips harder and he moved faster. Now. *Please.* Her core tightened as layer upon layer of tension built and spread and paralyzed her. *More.* She squeezed her eyes closed, envisioned that moment of release. So close. So close. Russ shifted and—*whoosh*—the release came, all bright lights and soaring happiness. She focused on the perfection of it, *savored* it, wanting never to forget the euphoria of her and Russ together. She'd known it would be this way. *Knew it.*

Russ cried out and she looked up, watched him throw his head back, the muscles in his shoulders bunching as he took that same euphoric ride. She ran her fingers along the angles of his face, down his neck and across his shoulder, gently stroking until he collapsed on top of her.

Yes, they were good together. Case closed.

Eventually, Russ rolled off her, wrapped his arm around her waist and brought her into his side. With his free hand, he smacked his forehead. "Hot damn."

Penny snuggled into his side, curling her leg around his, wanting only to get closer. How was it that they'd just gotten as close as two people could—literally—and still it wasn't enough?

Maybe it was just him and the way he reminded her not everything was her fault.

"Thank you," she said.

He glanced down at her, his brows drawn. "Uh—"

Oh, no. He thought she was thanking him for the sex. Which she should probably do, but—ew—how cheesy. And horrific.

Playfully, she shoved him away. "Not for that. Pig."

"Hey, you're the one who said thank-you after I just sent you flying."

"Oh, please."

Russ grinned at her. "Just saying."

"If you weren't so damned arrogant, I'd say something nice, but forget it. I'm not doing it."

But once again, she snuggled into him, enjoying the banter and the ease between them. Russ had an ego for sure, but he didn't take every comment as a personal affront or an implied message. He let her be snarky without feeling offended. A lot of men wouldn't. In her experience, some men couldn't handle her direct manner and she'd often found herself apologizing for something she'd said.

For being herself.

Not a place a woman should find herself. And somehow, with Russ, she never did.

"Anyway," she said, "thank you for making me believe not everything is my fault. That's what I was thanking you for."

He rolled on top of her, the warm skin of his legs brushing hers, the connection sparking again. He kissed her softly, his lips skimming hers, no fury or urgency. Apparently, Russ liked slow lovemaking. Good to know.

"None of this is your fault," he said. "We're dealing with a psycho. There's no figuring him out. All we can do is wait for the next call and then catch him."

A knock sounded on her door—seriously?

In a quick move, Russ rolled to his feet. "And that would be our techy guy to go up on your phone line."

He smacked her on the hip. "Get dressed, babe. I'll answer the door."

RUSS TUCKED HIS SHIRT in while walking to the door. The knock sounded again, but he stopped, glanced in the mirror hanging next to the door, flattened his hair and adjusted the knot on his tie. Close enough. If he looked too primped, after the day he'd had so far, they'd definitely know something was up.

He checked the peephole and suddenly needed to urinate. Not wanting to waste any more time, he swung the door open.

Gerald Hennings stared a second, his gaze focused but perhaps unsure. A man who hadn't expected to see another man opening his daughter's door. Hennings blinked, then did it again, and that fast, Russ was a teenager picking up his date for prom.

Play this cool. Sure, he'd just gotten to know the man's daughter in a carnal way that made him want to howl, but he was still an adult. An FBI agent working a case.

"Afternoon, sir." Russ stepped back. "Penny is in the other room. I thought you were one of the tech guys from my office."

Penny's father stepped over the threshold and immediately swung back to Russ. "What's happened? She sounded upset. Told me to meet her here, and she doesn't do that in the middle of the day."

"Yes, sir. We have news for you."

"Dad?"

Both men angled to the hallway. Penny stood there, all Killer Cupcake in her spiked heels and a fresh suit. Any average Joe would be impressed. But Russ saw the stress in her puffy eyes and sullen face. This pain was too deep, too cutting, too *wrecking* even for Killer Cupcake after a round of mind-blowing sex.

"Honey," Gerald said, stepping toward her. "What is it?"

Gerald wrapped his arms around her and she held on, gripping his immaculate suit jacket in her fist. That fist—the desperate clutch of it—told the tale. Stiffness filled Russ's neck. He rolled his head, considered turning away. Giving them a minute of privacy and yet, he couldn't. Penny was about to destroy her father, and for the life of him, Russ couldn't fix that.

He cleared his throat. "We should sit."

Hennings stepped back—one giant step—and squared his shoulders. Physical preparation. The attempt to steel himself for a rough encounter. Russ knew about physical preparation. Nothing would prepare the man for this.

Hennings hitched up his pants at the thighs and sat on the sofa. Slowly, she parked herself across from him and looked up at Russ. He met her gaze and nodded, trying to offer encouragement. Then he held a finger to his chest, asking her if she'd like him to do it.

Her father swung his gaze between them. "Someone tell me."

Penny sat tall, swept her now-perfect blond hair—the hair he'd riffled his fingers through not ten minutes ago—over her shoulders and faced her father. "Dad, I'm sorry."

"For what?"

She shook her head, shut her eyes and her shoulders dipped. *Ah, Penny.* Russ sat on the arm of Penny's chair, set a hand on her shoulder. "Sir, Penny received a call earlier. I'm sorry to tell you this, but Zac has been kidnapped."

Gerald Hennings looked like a man who'd been shot. Stunned by an assault so fierce that the body didn't quite register it. It would take a few seconds to absorb and then the agony, that bone-deep heartbreak, would hit.

"Kidnapped," he said.

Penny leaned forward, grabbed her father's hand. "I'm so..."

She sucked in air, dropped her head, and her face contorted. The lines in her skin deepened as she let out the first sob.

Russ squeezed her shoulder and glanced back at Hennings. His body bowed backward and he slumped into the chair, his hand slipping from Penny's and falling to the sofa. At the loss of contact, Penny's mouth dropped open.

Ah, dang it. Russ knew exactly where her mind had gone. Always blaming herself.

Gerald let out a gasp mixed with a whimper.

"Dad?"

"Sir," Russ said. "We're on it. My office, along with the marshal service. We'll find him. Whatever it takes."

Now sobbing, Penny leaped over to sit next to her father and wrapped her arms around him. "I'm so sorry. I'm so sorry."

"I...I..." He looked up at Russ with watery eyes.

Still, he patted Penny's shoulder and Russ's respect for the man went to epic heights. After hearing this news, Hennings had the focus to comfort his daughter while his mind adjusted to the emotional trauma of his child being abducted.

As nutty as they were, the love these people shared was simply amazing. Russ's relationship with his own parents was strong, but not to this intensity. This unconditional acceptance. Suddenly, Russ wanted to be brought into that fold.

Somehow, in the course of a lifetime, Penny's oldest brother didn't appreciate what it took Russ just days to recognize.

He supposed jealousy did that to people. Blinded them, turned them hard and unyielding. Exactly how David was with Penny. Always blaming her for whatever infraction he perceived she'd committed.

"It's Heath, sir," Russ said, trying to fill air. "He grabbed him coming out of the courthouse today."

"Zac's alive?"

Penny finally sat back, threw her hands over her lips while staring at Russ.

"As far as we know."

Gerald glanced at Penny, looped his arm around her shoulders. "It's not your fault. Okay? Don't let your mind go there. I need you now."

Penny shot straight and lifted her chin. *Take a note.* The big guy had the magic bullet with his daughter.

"Good girl," Hennings said. "Does your mother know?"

"No. I wanted to tell you first."

"Good. I'll need to tell her. And Emma."

Emma. Zac's girlfriend.

Penny jabbed her fingers into her forehead. "How could I forget Emma?"

"I'll take care of it," her father said. He glanced at Russ. "I need details. Then I have to tell my wife."

"Of course. We have agents en route. I'll get someone to take you home and he can fill you in on the drive."

"No. He's watching. He said no FBI."

Russ turned back to her, cocked his head. "Penny, this is what we do. They won't see us."

Hennings ran his hands over his gelled hair, held them on top of his head for a minute before dropping them. Slowly, as if pulled by a string, he sat tall, reset his shoulders. Now Russ knew where Penny had learned her lessons in control.

"When is Heath making contact again?" Hennings asked.

"I'm not sure. Probably soon," Penny said. "He wants me to trade Elizabeth for Zac."

"Dear God."

"Dad, I wish I could go with you to tell Mom. We should do it together."

"No. You need to be here. Take the call from Heath. Zac is the priority. Everything we do now is about him. Understand?"

"Yes."

Russ waved Hennings toward the door. "No one is trading anyone. We'll find Heath. Every law-enforcement department in this city is looking for him. There's nowhere to run."

Chapter Fourteen

Penny watched her father—her *broken* father—leave. Yes, he'd pulled it together, but she'd spent countless hours in court and at home studying him. All in her quest to hone her skills and become an exceptional attorney. Just like him. She knew his moods, understood the jerky movements of his body language. His pinched lips added the final indicator that her father's world had just been shattered.

And instead of blaming herself, she needed to glue that world back together.

Somehow she'd get Zac back. She turned toward the door Russ had closed behind him and picked up her phone. Promise or no promise, her brother's life was now very much compromised. A game changer. Time to bring in her own investigators.

He'll hate you for this.

No way around it. Not when the FBI couldn't locate Colin Heath. A private investigator could move in ways the FBI couldn't. Bend a few laws, pressure witnesses, forego warrants for every damned thing.

The FBI could not.

Without a doubt, they needed help.

Penny stared at the door, waiting for Russ to return, and absorbed the weight of what she wanted to do. It would break her promise. Something she'd prided herself on not doing.

This went beyond a broken promise. Her family could be destroyed and Emma's heart broken.

She couldn't let any of that happen.

The front door swung open. She faced Russ, squared herself for battle. He narrowed his eyes. Already suspicious. How well he knew her already.

"Your dad is on his way."

Russ continued to stare at her, analyzing, looking for the tell. "Stop staring at me."

"Tell me I can trust you."

They'd just made love, maybe she'd considered it stress reduction at the time, but they both knew their relationship had changed because of it. There was meaning there now. The act itself was important and not just a one-off.

All her emotional walls had been battered today. "Can we not do this? Please?"

He waited a moment, rubbed one hand across his mouth, then let it fall to his side. "We'll get this guy. There's nowhere for him to go. I'm doing everything I know how to do."

"I know you are. And I love that about you."

"But?"

This might be her chance. "Sometimes it's not about us and what we can do. Sometimes it's about rectifying a situation. My brother's life is on the line. This is more than a case to me.

"I know that."

"Yes, but do you *understand* it?"

He puffed out his cheeks, let the air burst free. "Damn it."

This was it. She rushed toward him. "Listen to me. I have resources that can help us. Put yourself in my place. What if this were your mother or father?" His head snapped back. "Exactly. Wouldn't you want to do everything you could?"

"You want your investigator on this."

"I know we agreed not to, but that was before. This is different."

Something from the hallway bumped against the wall and he jumped, reached for his sidearm. "I need to check that."

"Russell? Please. Let me do this."

He marched toward the door, his suit jacket flapping as he walked. A man on a mission. "Do it. I don't want to know about it. Nothing."

Yes. "Thank you. I'll keep you out of it."

BY THE TIME Russ reentered the apartment, he had two technical agents in tow. Technical agents set up the phone intercepts to monitor all calls into the residence. Penny stood in the corner of the room, her back to the wall, arms folded, fingers gouging into her arms as she watched the men unload equipment.

"Gentlemen," Russ said, "this is Penny Hennings. Penny, this is Ron Turner and Josh Gayner. They'll be assisting."

Hellos were exchanged, hands were shaken and the men got to doing what they did best while Penny attempted not to look spooked.

And damn if he didn't want to wrap her in his arms and tell her he'd take care of it. That she had nothing to worry about. Egotistical? Sure. But he wanted to be the man who made things right in Killer Cupcake's world.

Bum luck that Penny and the most important case of his career were solidly intertwined.

He focused on Penny leaning against the wall, taking it all in with eyes that lacked her normal fire. Dead eyes. Not something he ever wanted to see.

Heath had ripped this woman's life apart, and so far all Russ had been able to do was watch. He breathed in. Time to stop watching.

"Guys," he said, "we don't have an exact time on the next call. Could be soon."

"We'll be ready," Ron said. "No problem there." He glanced at Penny and held up a cordless phone. "We're replacing your phone with this one."

Penny nodded, but by her drawn, pale face and spacey eyes, Russ's guess was she didn't have a clue what she was agreeing to. Didn't matter.

A shrill *bling* filled the room, followed by a rattle on the coffee table. Penny's cell phone. She leaped for it, fumbling it with shaking hands.

Russ held his arms out. "Relax. He said he'd call on the other line."

Penny checked the screen. "Blocked number. He always calls on a blocked number."

Hell. They'd already gone to a judge for emergency authority to track the calls into Penny's cell phone; Russ just wasn't sure if the judge had signed off yet. If not, they were set up on the wrong phone. "Answer it. Put it on speaker."

Penny pressed the button. "Hello?"

"It's me."

Male voice. Sounded like Zac.

"Zac?" Penny shrieked.

"I'm fine," he said, his voice firm, maybe more hoarse than usual.

Fatigue.

Or they beat the hell out of him.

"Oh, Zac. I'm so sorry. So sorry."

Crashing sounds erupted from the other end. Phone falling?

"I'm sure." This from another male voice.

Heath.

"That's your proof of life," he said. "I will contact you tomorrow morning. Be ready to hand over Elizabeth or your brother dies."

"Wait. Where will you call me?"

"I'll find you."

The line went dead.

Russ spun to the surveillance guys. Kidnappings were their specialty. "What the hell is he doing?"

"Buying time," Ron said. "Any idea for what?"

"No. If anything, he'd want to speed it up. The longer he gives us, the more time we have to find him. And pump information out of our witness."

A FEW MINUTES shy of 7:00 p.m., Penny rode the elevator to her office with Brent by her side. Needing to distract herself until Heath's next call, she decided work might be a welcome relief. Uselessly sitting in her apartment while the FBI swarmed the city in search of her brother would drive her insane, and Russ had no intention of letting her help. Too dangerous, he'd said.

Aggravating man.

Still, there'd been progress. As expected, Randy Jones had, in almost record time, given up his brother as the courthouse shooter. So much for family loyalty. The only problem was the brother had disappeared right along with Heath.

And since Russ wouldn't accept Penny's help, she'd done the only thing she could and scheduled a meeting with one of the firm's full-time investigators.

She glanced at Brent, who leaned against the side wall staring up at the blinking numbers as the elevator climbed. With nothing to say, Penny went back to her distorted image in the metal doors. Or maybe that stretched mess resembling her body being pulled in both directions was really her. Russ on one side and her family on the other. All wanted the case to be over, but for very different reasons.

If only they could all have their wishes. Catching Colin Heath would do that. Only, the man was making it difficult. And one thing Penny didn't like was difficult people.

The elevator dinged and Brent held his arm out. "I know," Penny said. "You first."

Thankfully, their ride over had been quiet. No inquiries from him regarding this late visit to her office after her brother had been violently snatched off the street. Even if Brent had asked, she wouldn't provide any information.

Not about this meeting.

This meeting would hopefully bring her closer to Zac.

Penny handed her key card to Brent, who swiped it at the entrance to Hennings & Solomon. After six, the place went on lockdown. Something that, in the past, irritated her because she'd always forgotten her key card. Now? No complaints.

Inside, Brent cleared the first office, then the others in the corridor. Penny waited, only slightly agitated that her life had become a series of starts and stops that left her no further than she'd been the day—two days even—before.

"You're good," Brent called.

She stepped into the hall, where he stood just outside her office door. "Thank you. I have a meeting with Jenna Hayward. She's an employee. She'll have a key."

Any further details regarding Jenna's employment would remain untold. For all Brent knew, Jenna might be another attorney rather than the firm's drop-dead-gorgeous private investigator. A former Miss Illinois, Jenna knew how to use her physical assets to get the Hennings & Solomon crew whatever they needed.

Penny hoped that trend would continue with this assignment.

Leaving Brent in the hallway, she slipped off her suit jacket, ditched the stilettos and folded up the sleeves of her blouse. She rolled her neck, let her head hang for a second, hoping the stretch might relieve the blinding throb slamming into her skull. No good. Exhaustion did that to her.

She collapsed into her desk chair and inhaled. *Focus on Zac.* Pushing through the fatigue would be the only way to get her brother back. To restore her family. Give her parents the gift of their middle child.

As of thirty minutes ago, her mother had been medicated. The heartache had been too fierce, and fearing a total breakdown, Mom's doctor had made the rare house call and administered a sedative.

Got any to share, Doc?

Someone knocked and Penny swiped at the tears threatening to tumble. She glanced up to see Jenna at the door in a black leather dress that looked more dominatrix than investigator. Her long sable hair hung loose and her lips curved into a smile as she nodded toward Brent. Brent didn't seem to mind the view of Jenna's backside.

"Big boy," she said.

"He is indeed. Close the door."

As she closed the door, Jenna offered Brent a finger wave. "Bye, sweetheart."

Penny let out a long breath. Then again, this was why they'd hired Jenna. She had power and a fearlessness that Penny admired and, at this moment, craved.

"You look awful," Jenna said.

"I know."

"I'm sorry about Zac." She sat in one of the guest chairs and dug her battered calfskin notebook from her purse. "Tell me what I can do."

"Colin Heath." Penny pulled a folder from her desk drawer and handed it to Jenna. "This is everything I have on him. Please photocopy that file and give it back to me. I need you to help us find him. I don't care what it costs. Dad is giving us carte blanche."

Jenna lips puckered. "This is the guy who has Zac?"

To keep her hands busy, Penny folded them on the desk. "Yes. We find him and my guess is we find my brother. He wants me to swap one of my clients for Zac."

"Ouch."

"That's putting it mildly. He says he'll contact me again in the morning, but I don't know when or by what means. He said he'd find me."

"Will the feds share their info?"

She thought back to Russ and his insistence that he not know any details regarding her investigator. "No. This is just us."

Jenna nodded. "Sure. I love cleaning up fed messes."

For a brief second, Penny considered that statement. "The lead on this is Russ Voight. He's an excellent agent. One I trust." *And just made love to.* "If Zac's safety weren't involved, I'd let the FBI—with Russ as the lead—handle it. Zac's a deal breaker for me."

"Understood." Jenna rose. "I'll get on this now. See what I can dig up. I have some friends in the finance world." She grinned. "A few owe me favors and they may know Heath."

"Which is why I adore you."

Jenna leaned over the desk, squeezed Penny's hand. "You know I'll do whatever I can. Whatever deal needs to be made, I'll make it and get you information."

Penny stared up at the beautiful Jenna and didn't doubt any of what she'd said. Still, the words bounced around in a hollow place in Penny's chest. Only Zac coming home would fill that space.

"Thank you," she said.

Jenna marched out of the office and, sensing Penny needed alone time, closed the door behind her.

Whatever deal needs to be made, I'll make it. Coming from Jenna, it sounded so confident. So righteous. Maybe it was. Maybe Penny was too deep into this to know.

So much trust had been put into the FBI, into Russ. Penny believed in his abilities, but he had to play by the rules. As an attorney, she understood the boundaries of the law. In Heath's criminal mind, boundaries were meant to be tested. In Russ's mind, and Penny's, they were forced to work within them.

Whatever deal needs to be made, I'll make it.

Penny rocked back in her chair, rolled her head from side to side. Trapped in the middle of this was Elizabeth and her son. So many lives at stake. Lives in Penny's care. Immense pressure.

If she could come up with a way to keep Elizabeth and little Sam safe *and* get Zac back, this thing might work out.

Capturing Heath would make the scenario perfect, but he'd managed to be a tough opponent.

At some point, she'd handed Heath control. She wasn't sure when, but slowly, he'd seized power.

Take it back. Right now. Take it back.

Penny sat forward. She needed to get ahold of Colin Heath. Quickly. And dummy her, she'd failed to mention it to the person who could make that happen. She picked up her desk phone and dialed Jenna's cell. "Hi. Sorry. I forgot something. There's a man named Simon Caldwell. He's in prison. Murdered my client's husband. There are notes on him in the file. I need to get a message to Colin Heath. I think Simon will know how to find him."

"Oh, goody," Jenna said. "I'm on it. If I can get to him, what's the message?"

"Just tell him I have an offer Heath can't refuse."

RUSS STOOD IN THE HALLWAY outside Penny's apartment, waiting for her and Brent to come up the elevator. Only nine o'clock and it felt as if he'd been awake for three days. The smell of cooking meat lingered in the hallway and his stomach rumbled. When had he last eaten? Not lunch. He'd skipped that. He thought. Who knew?

Colin Heath. This guy was the biggest pain in the chops he'd faced. Next to Penny, of course. Penny at least was a fun pain. She challenged him, made him crave verbal swordplay. Not to mention the physical aspects they'd explored. The fact that she enjoyed it just as much wasn't lost on him. What that said about them, he wouldn't analyze.

Right now, he wanted to get his eyes on that compact body of hers and strip her naked.

Again.

Another issue because they had Zac Hennings being held hostage somewhere and Russ needed to think about that particular Hennings. Not the one currently consuming him.

From the middle of the hallway, the elevator dinged—finally. Brent stuck his giant head out, and for some reason, Russ found it funny.

Damn, I'm tired. Why else would he find Brent's head sticking out of an elevator amusing? He shook his head, jammed his knuckles into his eyes and rubbed. "You're clear."

Brent stepped into the hallway. "What's funny?"

Your enormous head. "Nothing."

And then Penny—his daily dose of torment—walked toward him on her stilt shoes and…and…Brent who?

For such a tiny woman, Penny knew how to command space. Her navy suit, the one she'd changed into after they'd explored various erogenous zones, somehow still looked neat and pressed. As she neared, he spotted the dark shadows under her eyes.

"Hello, Russell," she said in a tone that warned him they had company and whatever thoughts he'd employed needed to be suppressed.

"Hello, Penny."

He turned to her apartment door and unlocked it with the key she'd left him in case he needed to get back in.

"You checked the apartment?" Brent wanted to know.

"Yeah. She's good."

Penny turned to Brent. "Thank you for everything today."

"No problem. Try to rest. It'll be a long day tomorrow."

"I will." She glanced at Russ, their eyes connected for half a second, but not enough for Brent to look sideways at, and nodded. "Good night, gentlemen."

"Good night. I'll keep you posted."

"Thank you."

With Penny inside the apartment, Russ focused on Brent. If possible, Brent appeared in worse shape than Russ. His hair stuck up in various places, the wrinkles in his suit looked three days old and his tie knot hung loose. "You're a disaster."

"I know."

They'd both been dealing with Penny's saucy mouth and stubbornness for days now, and as much fun as it provided, the woman's energy could take the toughest of men down.

"When are you off?"

"Another hour. The third-shift guy was working a lead on Zac. I told him I'd stay later."

A lead. At this point he'd take anything, considering he'd just spent three hours hunting down Heath's family members. "Something good?"

"I don't know. Someone saw a white van on the South Side. Million white vans on the South Side. He's probably chasing his tail."

"Never know." Russ propped a shoulder against the wall and jerked his chin toward the door. "How is she?"

"Distracted."

Interesting answer. Not upset, not hysterical, not quiet. Distracted. What Russ needed to know, but wouldn't ask, which was a problem because the FBI agent in him would be all over it, was if Penny was distracted because her brother had been kidnapped or because she was up to something.

Whatever the issue, when Russ stripped away the layers, he and Penny had a beast inside them. It was part of his attraction to her. They understood each other. The beast kept them curious and strong and fighting. And if Russ had a brother who'd been kidnapped, the beast for damn sure wouldn't tolerate waiting. The beast would be planning.

The fact that he didn't fully trust her bothered him. Or maybe what bothered him was the hit his ego took because Penny wanted her own investigator hunting Heath.

He'd talk to Penny. Just to remind her they'd made a deal involving her client becoming a cooperating witness and he expected her to stick to that deal. No matter what.

"Why don't you take off? I've got Penny. I need to talk to her anyway. I'll wait for the next guy."

Brent scratched his head. “You sure?”

“Yeah. You look beat. And she’ll need you sharp tomorrow.”

“I like her. She’s high maintenance, but she’s funny. Makes me want to help her. You know?”

“Trust me. I know. She tore into me on the stand once and somehow I didn’t mind.”

Brent laughed. “I could see that.”

“Go home.”

Russ waited for Brent to step on the elevator, then knocked lightly on Penny’s door. The snick of the lock sounded and she swung the door open, wearing a bright pink tank top—no bra this time—and a pair of running shorts. The sheer lack of sex appeal in that outfit made it all the more erotic.

He took one long perusal of her body and zeroed in on her breasts. He needed her in a bed in the next five minutes. Forget the talk. And everything else. “You need to stop opening the door in these getups. I could have been Brent.”

“I heard you tell him to leave.” She batted her eyes. “I was listening, *Russell*.”

“You’re a witch.”

She stepped back and waved him in. “Flattery will get you everywhere. Now tell me about my brother.”

“Nothing new. Not yet. We’re working some informants, though, and they’ve given us locations to check. You never know. How are you holding up?”

“You know, I don’t think Heath will hurt Zac. It occurred to me that he needs me. If he…” She closed her eyes, threw her shoulders back and opened her eyes again. “If he hurts my brother, I can unleash Elizabeth. He knows I have evidence that will put him in prison. He won’t risk my wrath.”

Let’s hope.

“You could be right.”

“You don’t think?”

He shrugged. “I don’t make predictions. I want to believe you’re right, though. It’s logical. And you’re smart.”

"And you want sex."

He grinned. "There is that."

"Except something is on your mind. I can tell."

"Aside from your brother being kidnapped and that I licked every inch of your body this afternoon, which scares the hell out of me because I've never done that before."

"Licked a woman's body?" she cracked.

"Jokes? Really?"

She stepped closer, ran her hands up his chest and settled them on his shoulders. "You're thinking too much."

"I've got a few things on my mind. One of which is trying not to blow this case because I've gotten emotional about the stubborn defense attorney." He slid his arms around her waist. "I hate defense attorneys."

"I know you do. I'm sorry."

He needed to ask her if he could trust her. Once again make her say it. To remind her she'd promised.

Except she inched closer, pressed her breasts against him and wrapped her hand around the back of his neck. *I'm dead.* Whether the fatigue had softened him, he didn't know, but there was definitely one place that had stayed hard. And that place knew exactly where it wanted to be. And it wasn't discussing whether or not he could trust Penny.

Who needed trust?

"Will you stay with me tonight?"

"Can't."

She stuck out her bottom lip and he laughed. "Another marshal will be here in an hour. How will it look if I walk out of here tomorrow morning?"

"Didn't think of that. I hate babysitters. It's stifling."

He leaned down, dropped a kiss on her pouty lips. Too cute. "I know. And I'm sorry. It'll be over soon."

"Russell?"

"What?"

"I think I love you."

The words came at him, moving slow, then a muffled

roar echoed in his head. *Blood rush.* His vision blurred and he blinked a couple of times. *Hang on here.*

What was she doing? She *loved* him? That statement might make him the luckiest man alive, but chances were this sudden lovefest was a reaction to the nightmare of the past few days. Penny needed a safe place to land and it looked as if Russ was it. He couldn't blame her, either. With the mess surrounding her, he'd run for cover, too.

"Penny—"

She pressed two fingers over his lips. "Don't say anything. Whatever this is or isn't, we don't need to talk about it. I need my brother back. Once that happens, we'll talk. Right now, I want you to take me to bed and remind me of why life is good. Will you do that for me?"

Uh, yeah. At least, his body said yes. The brain—the one that counted here—said no. Sex right now would only feed this illusion that she loved him. And no doubt it was an illusion. He'd seen this hundreds of times throughout his career. When life sucked, people imagined themselves in love.

Penny tugged lightly on his shirt and he stared down into her big blue eyes, ran his fingers over her perfect cheekbone and his chest broke open. She did that to him. Every time he looked at her, touched her, it filled emptiness.

Eventually, she'd figure out she didn't love him. Not the way she thought she did. Not the way he wanted her to.

Eventually.

She tugged his shirt again, inched closer and rested her head against his chest. *I'm sunk.* At this moment, selfish creep that he was, he'd let her believe it.

Done deal. No more thinking required. He grinned. "Well, if you insist. There might be a few places I missed licking this afternoon."

Chapter Fifteen

After an intolerably long night, Penny sat at her desk, scrolling through emails, wanting nothing more than communication from Jenna or Colin Heath. Anything that would make the loss of sleep last night worthwhile. Of course, Russ had done a fine job of distracting her for a bit. At least until the other marshal showed up and they couldn't come up with a decent excuse for Russ to be lingering. Other than her simply wanting him there.

And, of course, she'd told him she loved him. *Stupid girl.* By now, with all the cases she'd worked, she should know emotions were trouble after traumatic situations.

You should know better.

Time for that later. Once Zac came home and Heath was behind bars. Then she and Russ could figure out what exactly they were doing with each other.

Assuming he was still speaking to her. If the idea she had brewing worked, Russell Voight would despise her. Part of her hoped he'd understand the desperation involved, but with his stubbornness, he'd see an end run to Heath as a betrayal.

She couldn't blame him. She'd given her word she'd cooperate, which she'd done.

Until they lost Zac.

She flicked the computer mouse away and sat back. Two hundred emails waited for her while she obsessed over her plan, one that might not even be put into action if she couldn't get a message to Heath. All this worrying wouldn't help. She simply had to move forward, wait for Heath to contact her and hope to whatever force might actually be on her side that the FBI found her brother.

Alive.

Jenna swung in the door wearing a short floral skirt and halter top that shouted "I'm in shape and can kick butt." Probably not the most appropriate office attire, but Penny had settled that in her mind long ago. As long as Jenna kept the information flowing, there'd be no friction regarding her clothing choices.

She dropped a file on the desk and lowered herself into one of the guest chairs. "How much do you love me?"

"I love you a lot. Maybe more than I did yesterday."

"Excellent answer." She flipped open the file. "Found you a guy who found you a guy who found you a guy."

"Three guys?"

"Maybe four. I lost track. I've been at this all night and you'll stroke out when you see what it cost me, but you said no limit." Jenna dug a cell phone from her giant Louis Vuitton tote. "When this phone rings. Answer it."

Penny stared at it. "Who will it be?"

"If I'm any good at my job, which we both know I am, it should be our boy Colin. Or at least someone close to him. You give him whatever message you want and my work here is done."

Found him. Maybe the obsessing paid off. Penny sat forward and reached for the phone. "When will he call?"

"Not sure. I told my contact you wanted to speak with him privately." She gestured to the phone. "On that phone. Where no one else—the FBI included— could possibly know about the call."

"Whose phone is this?"

"Mine. Disposable. I gave them the number."

"Okay."

Jenna smacked her hands against the arms of the chair. "Anything else?"

"No. I'm good. And thank you. This is excellent work."

Jenna didn't know it, but Penny would make sure there was a fat bump in her next paycheck. The woman may have just saved Zac's life.

RUSS STEPPED THROUGH the main door of Welberg Prison in Southeast Michigan and met the stale, antiseptic odor of a building that hadn't seen fresh air in thirty years. As an FBI agent, the smell of prisons wasn't foreign, but he never did get used to that caged-in feeling. Even if he wasn't the one caged.

After a three-hour drive made worse by morning traffic, his damned day was already out of control and not helping his mood. For a guy who liked a certain amount of chaos in his world, the current level had shot to the red zone. Heath, Zac, Penny. They were all one huge fireball rolling toward a dry forest owned by special agent Russell Voight.

Total mess.

After signing in and checking his weapon, an armed guard led Russ to a small conference room used by attorneys and other law-enforcement officers when they needed to interview witnesses. Or, in this case, convicted felons.

Russ noted the smack of his dress shoes against the cement floor, but didn't look down. As a general rule, he kept his head high—no sign of weakness or fear—when visiting a prison. Even if the bare white walls and the sense of isolation scared the hell out of him.

The guard deposited Russ, closed and locked the door behind him and hightailed it to retrieve Russ's interviewee. Jamming his hands into his pockets, Russ surveyed the room. More scrubbed white walls. Plenty of that around here. In the middle of the room, a metal table sat bolted to the floor so no daredevil convict could use it as a weapon. Along with the table came two plastic chairs that, if upended, would most likely break before they did any damage. No muss, no fuss.

He remained standing, refusing to sit until the prisoner was cuffed to the table. Another self-imposed rule. Sitting would allow the prisoner to loom over him, to assume the power role, when he entered the room. Russ never gave away power.

Never.

In his head, he reviewed his questions. Simon Caldwell had been convicted of murdering Elizabeth Brooks's husband. At the time, Caldwell had been employed by Colin Heath and by all accounts the two had been close. What that relationship was now, Russ didn't know, but he was about to lay out a carrot that Caldwell would be a fool to ignore.

All Caldwell needed to do was (a) help Russ locate Heath and (b) testify against the man. In exchange his sentence would be reduced to the minimum and he'd walk away from prison with another forty years of life ahead of him.

Or he could stay in prison for those forty years.

His call.

Russ hoped he'd make the smart choice. Then again, the fact that the guy was incarcerated didn't bode well for smart choices.

A loud buzz sounded from outside the room. *Here we go.* Russ rolled his shoulders, dragged his hands from his pockets and let them hang at his sides while he waited for Caldwell to enter.

The guard unlocked the door and opened it for the shackled prisoner. Caldwell's head had been shaved and he wore navy prison scrubs. On his feet were white canvas slip-ons. Not exactly a fashion statement, but in prison it was as good as they got. Caldwell's pale skin stretched over a long, thin face and indicated the sallow look of someone who hadn't seen sunlight in months. His build wasn't big, but he had a height advantage of a couple of inches.

Still, Russ wasn't the one trussed like an animal.

"Chains stay on," the guard said as Caldwell took the chair by the wall.

The guard cuffed the prisoner to a hook on the table, then left. Once the door closed, Russ took the seat across from Caldwell.

Caldwell smirked. As if sitting in a cell was more interesting than meeting with the FBI. People.

"I'm special agent Russ Voight. FBI. I'm here regarding Colin Heath."

He shrugged. "I'm popular today."

What now?

Wanting to engage his target in a casual manner, Russ relaxed his shoulders and kept his hands on his thighs. "Heath's been busy."

"I wouldn't know. But the broad who was here earlier was a lot better looking than you."

Russ's stomach dropped, but he didn't move. Instead, he focused on keeping his facial features and body language neutral. No weakness anywhere.

But if the "broad" was a petite blonde, Penny Hennings was in for one hell of a battle with him. After all the yapping he'd done about being able to trust her, she'd better not have sold him out. Professionally, it would be a disaster for him. Emotionally? He couldn't go there. Not when he'd spent all that damned time ignoring his own warnings about getting involved with the sassy defense lawyer.

"What broad?"

Caldwell stared out the miniscule window, where a slash of morning sunshine shone against the glass. "Jenna someone. She's an investigator from some law firm downtown."

The investigator. The one Russ had said he didn't want to know about. Suddenly, he wanted to know everything. "And she was here this morning?"

"Yep. Wanted to get in touch with Heath, figured I knew where to find him."

Russ thought about it. He and Penny *had* agreed she

could put her investigator on the case. Maybe she hadn't violated their agreement. Which would prolong her life.

"And do you?"

He shrugged. "I gave her some names. People who might know." He glanced out the window again. "Nice day out?"

Have I got a deal for you. "Best of the month. And one you'll miss because you're in here. I can change that."

Caldwell sat back, made a move to lift his shackled hands and gave up. *Bingo.* Russ rested his arms on the table. "Tell me where to find Heath, testify against him and you walk out of here after serving the minimum. I can make it happen."

"You want to *flip* me?"

"Or you can spend the rest of your life in this stink hole."

"Why's everyone so interested in Heath?"

"Outside of his total lack of respect for the law?"

Caldwell bellowed a laugh. One of those deep, gut-busting ones, and Russ wanted to pop him. Under the table, he tapped his foot. Five times. Enough to get rid of a little energy.

Tough spot here. Russ typically shared no information, but part of a good negotiation was the give-and-take. He'd give a little, maybe get a lot. "He may be facing a kidnapping charge. Not to mention murder, obstruction and anything else I can nail him with."

"The Brooks woman?"

No chance, ace. "What did you tell the investigator this morning?"

"Nothing. She wanted names. I gave her names."

"What'd you get out of it?"

"I got to stare at a beautiful woman in a low-cut shirt a few extra minutes. You'd be surprised how that motivates a man."

Not really. Not after he'd been lusting after Penny. When it came to his baser needs, Russ had no problem understanding the effect of a beautiful woman.

"Besides," Caldwell continued, "she said she had a message for Heath. How she expected me to deliver it, who knows?"

"What message?"

"All she said was her boss had a deal for him. One he couldn't refuse."

Knew it. What the hell was Penny up to? Still, information from a prisoner had to be vetted. For all he knew, this deal Penny wanted to make could be nonsense. A ploy to find Heath.

"Plenty of deals to be had today," Russ said. "Give me the names you gave to Jenna-the-beautiful, answer my questions regarding Heath and testify when I lock him up, and you walk out of here ahead of schedule. Way ahead. Are you in or out?"

"Dude, if I talk to you, it won't matter when I'm released—I'll be dead anyway. Heath won't let me live to testify. Look what happened to Sam Brooks."

Russ had anticipated this. "We'll get you moved to a safer facility."

"And what? Isolation? Being by myself all day? Bad enough I'm in the joint, never mind not having anyone to talk to. I'll go out of my mind. No deal. Not unless I walk out of here today and go into witness protection."

Russ was good, but not that good. Still, he wasn't ready to give up. "Let me see what I can do."

Again, Caldwell smirked. "I'm not going anywhere."

BY NINE-THIRTY Penny had nearly lost her mind. Two hundred emails cleared. Not bad. Of course, she'd arrived at the office at six-thirty in hopes that Heath would call early with instructions on Zac. Heck, she'd hoped her instincts were right about him calling her office instead of the house. Now she wanted a call from him not only regarding Zac, but to possibly make a side deal with him via Jenna.

Slowly, she'd begun to figure him out. He wanted to keep

her on edge, which meant calling different phones. Her best guess was the office line would be next in the rotation.

Three hours she'd been waiting and no call. Not even on her cell. What if he'd called the house?

No. She'd be aware. The feds were monitoring that phone as well as the office phone. All areas covered. She'd just have to wait. Maybe return some calls while she did.

She reached for the handset just as the cell phone Jenna had given her rang. Blocked number. *Him.*

Penny held her breath, stared at her closed office door. Brent was right outside. She could bring him into this, but then she'd never know if her plan would have worked. And Zac's life was the priority. The phone rang. *Relax.* She hit the button. "Hello?"

"Good morning, lovely Penny. I heard you were looking for me. Wanted a private chat."

She sure did. "Correct."

"And the FBI is not listening?"

"No. If I had them listening I wouldn't have spent a small fortune simply to get a message to you."

A vision of Russ smiling at her flashed in her mind. *He won't be smiling after this.* After this, he'd never smile at her again.

"Go ahead," Heath said.

She gripped the phone tighter, pictured Zac's face instead of Russ's. "I want my brother back. I think we can compromise. I won't turn Elizabeth Brooks over to you. I might as well kill her myself, because surely that's a death sentence. However, I will make sure she is not available to testify for the FBI. She will never again be an issue for you. I guarantee she will disappear. Vanish."

Silence drifted across the phone line.

"She's agreed to this?" he finally asked.

A fierce energy whipped into Penny, made her stomach churn. She stood, paced behind her desk and shook out her free hand. "All she wants is her child safe. If we guarantee that, she'll live with it."

"And you'll do this how?"

He's mine. Her stomach settled as all that whipping energy spurred her mind to action. "Not your concern. There is a catch, though. I will keep any evidence she has. And believe me when I say she's given me a boatload on you. If anything happens to Elizabeth or Sam, every scrap of that evidence gets handed over to the FBI. That's the deal. Elizabeth and her son disappear, Zac is released and you go about your life as a free man. As much as it kills me, I'll let you walk away if it'll save my brother, Elizabeth and Sam. But the evidence stays with me. Anything goes wrong, it all gets turned over."

"How do I know this isn't a setup?"

"You don't."

"Lovely Penny, I wish I'd hired you as my lawyer. But, alas, I was late to the party."

Penny bit back a snarky comment. "Deal or not?"

"Eh, why not? I have nothing to lose here."

Got him. Her shoulders dropped, a massive unloading of pressure. "I'll need time to speak with Elizabeth."

"You have five hours. I will contact you on this number at two-thirty. Be available or the deal is off."

"Fine."

Penny slapped down the phone and breathed in. She had five hours to figure out how to make Elizabeth disappear.

And avoid Russell Voight.

Chapter Sixteen

Penny, escorted by Brent, rode to the safe house with her head spinning. Should she tell Russ about this deal with Heath? Intellectually, she knew she should. Emotionally, she wasn't so sure. The man had ordered the murders of two people. Somehow she doubted he'd be afraid to carry out his threats against Russ and her family.

Watching the bobbing boats on the lake wasn't helping and she turned her gaze to the road in front of her. Racing thoughts aside, a serious lack of sleep left that tenth cup of coffee roiling in her stomach.

"Will you hate me if I puke in your car?"

Brent shot her a sideways glare and went back to the road. "Yes."

"Okay."

She eased back against the headrest. Only a few more minutes and they'd be there. At which point she'd tell the marshals she needed to speak with her client. Privately. She'd then convince Elizabeth to let the Hennings family create her a new life, with financial support, on a tropical island where she and her son would live quietly and without danger. One thing about being a criminal defense attorney, Penny and her coworkers had all sorts of contacts who knew how to make people become someone else.

In exchange for her new identity, Elizabeth would refuse

to testify against Heath and trust Penny to protect the massive amount of evidence she'd collected.

No problem.

Right.

For hours now, Penny had blocked out the rage she anticipated Russ would spew at her when he heard she'd double-crossed him. This was more than a professional betrayal. It would look as if she'd used him, and Russ, with his hatred of shifty lawyers, would never forgive that.

Ever.

She lowered the window and stuck her face out, let the moist lake air drench her. Slowly, she inhaled—*one, two, three*—then exhaled.

"Hey," Brent said. "Seriously, are you gonna puke?"

Maybe. "No. I'm exhausted and drank too much coffee. The combination is not good. I'm over-amped."

"I told you to stop with the coffee."

"Blah, blah. I know. But I'm running on fumes."

"And now you're sick on top of it."

She glanced over at him, and the big marshal shook his head. Although she appreciated his attentiveness, she could happily bludgeon him. "Brent, don't make me slap you."

He made a snorting noise as he hung the left on to the quiet lane that would lead them to the safe house.

Finally.

Five minutes later, Penny escorted Elizabeth outside, where they huddled behind a tree and three large bushes. Brent and the other marshal gave them enough space to speak privately but not enough where they couldn't react quickly.

"What's wrong?" Elizabeth asked. "Is it Zac?"

Perhaps motherhood had honed Elizabeth's senses, but the woman always knew when something had not gone according to plan.

"No. Not Zac." Penny checked behind her, ensuring Brent

and the other marshal were out of earshot. "I spoke to Heath this morning."

"Oh, no."

"Elizabeth, I don't know how to do this—"

"It's fine. Just say it."

"If I were to tell you that you wouldn't have to testify against Heath, and I'd get you a new life, in a place of your choosing, where you and Sam could live without fear, what would you say?"

Elizabeth's head snapped back. "Is this for real or hypothetical?"

"Does it matter?"

"I guess not."

Penny touched her arm, huddled closer. "Sam would be safe. Guaranteed."

"I wouldn't have to testify? Ever?"

"No."

Stepping back, Elizabeth turned toward the ancient oak tree and rested a shoulder against it. "Wow."

"It's a lot to absorb. We all have so much to lose."

Their gazes connected for a long moment. Elizabeth understood the strength of family and the heartbreak that came with loss. On some level, she and Penny shared the same fears about losing their loved ones. But Penny wouldn't rush her. Not much, anyway. She'd give her a few minutes to consider the offer. Hopefully, she wouldn't yell for one of the marshals and blow the whole deal to bits. Elizabeth glanced at the marshals—*please, no*—then came back to Penny.

"If you'd guarantee our safety, I guess I'd take that deal. But I can't believe after all this—" Elizabeth waved her arms toward the house "—Agent Voight would agree to that."

"He hasn't."

"Then what are we talking about?"

"*I* spoke to Heath. On my own. He wanted me to trade you for Zac."

Elizabeth's gaze hardened and the corners of her lips dipped as she processed the words.

Penny held up her hand. "I told him I couldn't do that. I told him if he agreed to my terms, which included me keeping all the evidence you've collected and him forgetting about you, I wouldn't turn anything over to the FBI. He wants to stay out of prison and this deal does that for him. I made the best deal I could. You and your son stay safe and I get my brother back."

"How can we trust him?"

"We can't. That's the risk. But my father has had a long career. He knows all sorts of people. Creating a new identity for you will not be a problem. You'd be forced to leave the country, though. The upshot is, you wouldn't have to testify and Heath would leave you alone. If you testify, even if he's convicted, you won't know a day of peace."

A hot wind blew and the leaves overhead rustled. Elizabeth stared up at them, thinking, then came back to Penny. "What about the witness-protection program?"

Penny had anticipated this. "We could work something out with the government and they'd send you wherever they chose. You would have no control. With Heath's deal, you have control."

"And your brother would be safe."

"Yes. I won't lie, I want you to take this deal, but there are downsides. The government will not take kindly to us wasting their time. At the very least, they'll send you to prison for the illegal trades you've admitted to."

Not to mention the career implications Penny herself would face. She didn't want to be known as the lawyer who reneged on a good deal with the feds.

Elizabeth sagged against the tree. "Wow."

"I know."

"Can I think about it?"

No. She couldn't think about it. No time for that. But the woman had just been thrown a new plan. A completely different one than she'd expected, and down deep, Penny knew what that felt like. The loss of her brother the day before had inflicted the same torment.

"We don't have a lot of time. Heath will be calling me again at two-thirty."

"That fast?"

"Yes."

"Penny, I know this is about Zac's safety and I want to say yes, but I have Sam to worry about. He's all I have left. I have to think about how this will impact him. I promise you I'll have an answer by two-thirty."

Penny's cell phone chirped. Russ's new ringtone. The one that set him apart from the bazillion other random people who endlessly called her. Also a reminder that she'd forgotten to remove the damned battery. *Stupid, Penny.* A dull throb bumped at her temples. She should answer it. But he may have heard she was at the lake house with Elizabeth and he'd want to know why. Explaining it couldn't be done over the phone. She was about to demolish his case and, if nothing else, he deserved to hear it in person.

Even if he'd despise her for it.

She squeezed her eyes closed, focused on Zac's safety and not the feel of her heart being torn in half. *Don't do this.* But what kind of life had she created that she had to choose between her brother and the one man who accepted her lunacy, her relentless schedule and her ambition? A man she could envision a future—a great future—with.

Russell Voight understood her. And she was about to lose him. Worse, she wouldn't blame him.

So confused.

The chirping stopped and she opened her eyes, focused on Elizabeth and saving her and her son. Bringing Zac home. Yes. That was what she needed to do. Go with the positives. In another minute, her voice mail would chime. She'd remove the phone's battery and call Russ later. After

Elizabeth gave her an answer. Then she'd know for sure if her plan would be put in motion and if she would have to admit to him what she'd done.

Chapter Seventeen

Penny swung into the office reception area and stopped. Just halted where she stood. Sitting in one of the ultramodern, sharp-angled red guest chairs the decorator went a little insane over was Russ. He casually flipped through a magazine and then, as if sensing her presence, looked up. In that look was nothing soft.

At least the flat line of his lips and his tight jaw gave that impression. In fact, he could cut through steel with that look. She slid her briefcase higher on her shoulder, squeezed the strap and plastered a smile on her face. "Well, hello."

With extreme care, Russ closed the magazine and gently laid it on the chrome end table. Penny hated chrome. She enjoyed traditional style with wingback chairs and sturdy mahogany tables. Those things brought comfort. Coziness.

Chrome, in Penny's mind, brought cold. Russ's menacing, laser glare only reinforced the feeling.

He was too quiet. Too *still.* Russ had a way about him. All confined energy and quick, purposeful movements. When he entered a room, a commanding presence came with him. She'd grown used to it. Drew safety from it.

This Russ? A tad scary.

He stood and faced her, his dark eyes narrowing only a fraction, but the look—suspicion—set her back. She wasn't ready for him. Not yet. Not when Elizabeth hadn't made her decision yet.

"Let's talk." He glanced at the nosy receptionist. "Privately."

"Of course. Any word on Zac?"

He tilted his head. "I'm hoping you can tell me."

He knows. She'd been careful. Or so she'd thought. But Jenna had said she'd been working all night talking to multiple sources. Maybe one of her informants leaked information to the FBI. Russ had connections everywhere and someone easily could have alerted him to Jenna's investigation. But Penny had told him she'd use an investigator from the firm to help, and good investigators worked their connections. Being a good investigator himself, he'd understand that.

She led him back to her office and glanced at her father's closed door. On the way from the lake, she'd used Brent's phone and called him. Her mother was still heavily sedated and finally calm. Dad, not so much. The stress had to be breaking him. At fifty-eight, her father still had the superior strength to take on the toughest of opponents, but this level of emotional trauma was unprecedented in their world.

Her oldest brother flying in wasn't making the situation any better. As much as she felt they needed to gather as a family, David would only create more tension. He'd also place the blame at Penny's feet, which she'd already spent an entire day doing. She didn't need David beating her up. She'd done a fine job on her own.

She unlocked her door and waved Russ in. "Have a seat."

"I'll stand."

She dropped her briefcase next to the desk and eyed his stiff posture, all that contained energy waiting to launch. The man was spoiling for a fight. "Fine. Stand. I'm tired and I'm sitting."

"Where've you been?"

Not ready for this. Still, she lowered herself into her

chair, sat back and squared her shoulders. "Russell, you're acting strange."

He rolled his bottom lip out, tilted his head again. His behavior alone, the quiet demeanor, told her he knew. Now she'd have to figure out just how *much* he knew.

"I drove out to Welberg first thing this morning."

Uh-oh.

"The prison?"

He folded his arms. "Don't. Even."

Caught.

"I met with Simon Caldwell. I had the genius thought that I'd flip him. Make him an offer."

I'll make him an offer he can't refuse. "What offer?"

"A reduced sentence if he told me where Heath was."

"I see," Penny said.

"I'm sure you do. Considering your investigator got to him before I did."

Penny swallowed, pushed her shoulders back another half inch. "You knew I was putting someone on it."

"I did. One thing I didn't realize was you had a message for Heath."

Penny stayed silent. Really, there was nothing else to do. At some point, she'd figure the odds of Russ and Jenna going to the same source within hours of each other. Later, it would seem reasonable. Right now, she wanted to climb to the roof and throw herself off.

"You're quiet," Russ said. "That's a switch."

The sarcasm, she could accept. She deserved nothing less.

"What have you done, Penny?"

She gripped her chair.

Russ finally moved away from the door and stepped closer. "Tell me what you did."

His voice held a menacing growl, as if every ounce of anger had been packed into a tight ball, waiting to be hurled at her. She wished he'd do it already. Just let loose. A yelling Russ, she knew how to handle. "I haven't done anything. Yet."

He folded his arms. Stared hard. "Tell me."

For a few seconds, they stayed in that locked battle of wills and Penny contemplated holding out. Her stubborn streak ran just as wide as Russ's. If it came down to it, they'd die of old age in this silence. Only, who else would die with them?

Jig's up. "I was going to tell you this afternoon. I swear to you."

"Liar."

"No. I was. I promised you, but this is different." She kept her gaze on his, intensely focused, hoping the truth would drill through his anger and he'd understand. "He's my brother."

Russ jerked his head. "You went around me. Because I'm the incompetent schmo that can't close this case."

Penny shot out of her chair and slapped her hand on the desk. "I never thought that. I had bargaining power. That's all."

"Tell me."

She bit her bottom lip. Desperately, she wanted to tell him. To confess it all and maybe everything would work out. But Zac needed her. Chancing it could risk his life. "I can't."

Russ's face flushed with the effort of controlling all that roiling anger. Finally, the Russ she knew. He jabbed a finger at her. "Damn you. Months of nonstop work, of digging and chasing leads and working eighty-hour weeks, and you do this?"

"Russell!"

"Screw you, Penny. You gave me your word. You *played* me."

He held his hands out, fingers slightly curled. Yes, he wanted to strangle her. She could see it. *Anger is okay.* He'd been angry before and forgiven her. She rushed around the desk, but he stepped back, putting distance between them. That distance was a knife plunging into her chest. She sucked in a breath, held it and tried to control her rupturing heart. "I'm sorry."

"Damn you."

He headed for the door, his steps hard against the thick carpet. *Stop him.*

"Russell!"

Brent stood in the hallway, eyebrows raised. "Problem?"

Russ kept moving. "If she tries to leave this office, arrest her."

Arrest? "Russell, I'm not chasing you."

"Guess what, babe?" he said without looking back. "I don't want you to. I can't stand to even look at you."

A small sound squeaked in her throat. *He's leaving.* She had to stop him. Make him understand. And just that fast, she ran to the hallway, her ankles wobbling on her heels as she did the one thing she swore she'd never do and chased down a man.

She pushed through a couple of associates gawking at her. *Go away.* Last thing she needed was an audience. Not that she had much choice. *Ignore them.* She got to Reception just as Russ stepped onto the elevator. "Russell. Please. Let me talk to you."

But the door began to close. Russ stood there staring at her, hatred pouring off him, and then, as if she were too hideous to see—too filthy to look at—he turned away.

The doors closed and Penny gasped. *He's gone.*

"Um, Penny?" the receptionist called.

Causing a scene in Reception hadn't been on the to-do list today and heat filled Penny's cheeks. *Way to go.* The boss's daughter making a mockery of herself.

She couldn't allow it. *Never let 'em see you sweat.* She eased her shoulders back, lifted her chin and spun to the receptionist. Brent stood beside the U-shaped desk, waiting for her to do something stupid. Like run. Well, why not? She could add it to the list of other stupid but necessary things she'd probably do while trying to save her brother.

The receptionist tapped her headset. "I have Elizabeth Brooks on the line for you. She says it's urgent."

Elizabeth. With an answer. Penny started toward her office. "Give me one minute and put her through."

After finding themselves on the disapproving end of Penny's scowl, the few associates who'd been rubbernecking in the hallway skulked back to their offices. She may have made an idiot out of herself, but she still had power around here. Even if she didn't feel it at the moment. *Get over it.*

She strode into her office, picked up the handset and waited for the line to ring. A few seconds later, line one lit up. She punched the button.

"Elizabeth?"

"Make the deal. Get your brother back. Sorry you had to wait on me."

Penny dropped into her chair, rested her head against her free hand. "It's okay. I know it was a big decision. You'll never know how sorry I am to put this on you."

"There's really no choice, is there?"

She wished there were. More than anything right now, she wanted to see Colin Heath rot in a cell. Instead, Brent strode into her office and planted himself in one of her guest chairs.

"I need to go. I'll call you soon."

She hung up and focused on Brent. "And what? You're going to sit there all day? I have clients to speak with. Attorney-client privilege and all that."

"I'll leave when you're talking. For now, you're not leaving my sight."

RUSS STEPPED INTO THE HOME of Gerald Hennings and took in the large curving staircase with the ornate brass railing leading to the second floor. The steps may have been marble. Russ wasn't sure and didn't care. All he cared about was the truckful of rage plowing through him, and if he didn't let it loose, he'd go insane.

Penny had shafted him. The woman had consumed his thoughts for months, but hell, off-the-charts sex shouldn't have been worth his career. *Defense lawyers. There you go.*

To the right of the entry, Hennings led him to a study where floor-to-ceiling bookcases lined one wall and upholstered furniture large enough to seat a dinosaur adorned the room. A rich man's office. A man whose wealth grew by getting criminals off. Colin Heath probably had an office like this. That thought only made Russ boil, so he turned his attention to Hennings.

In prior meetings, Hennings had been buttoned up tight. Expensive Italian suit, pocket square, fancy silk tie. The works. Today he wore khaki pants with a blue button-down shirt. Some would call it business casual. Russ's guess was this was about as casual as Gerald Hennings got.

Russ didn't wait for the man to sit. "I need to know what this deal is Penny made with Heath."

Hennings dropped into his desk chair and stared. "What deal?"

Yeah, as if he didn't know. Penny didn't make a move without her father knowing. "I'm giving you one shot to fill me in and maybe I won't have you both charged with obstruction. Start talking."

And now the big man straightened up and gave him a hard look. Angry. So what? Russ had anger in spades. He had enough anger to fill this mansion. Didn't matter.

"Watch your tone, Agent Voight. I don't know about any deal. I've been here with my wife all day. I spoke to my daughter earlier when she was on her way back from a meeting with Elizabeth."

This was news. "She met with Elizabeth this morning?"

"Yes. I assumed you were there." Hennings blew out a soft breath. "You think she met with Elizabeth about a deal with *Heath?*"

Either Penny made this move without her father or he was playing him right along with his daughter. But the high-pitched, shattered sound of shock in his voice didn't sound like an act. "I believe so."

Hennings leaned forward, snatched his phone up. "Let's find out."

PENNY KNEW BRENT had one serious problem. That being nature had made a call. An immediate one he refused to answer.

And Heath would be calling in fifteen minutes.

Bladders were only so big and she guessed by Brent's increased fidgeting that his was about to go boom.

"For heaven's sake," she said. "Go pee. You're making me nervous with all the damned squirming. I have calls to make, anyway."

He stared a minute and she sighed. "Suit yourself. It's your exploding bladder."

Finally, he stood, pointed a beefy finger at her. "I've been good to you these last few days."

"Yes, you have."

"If you move from this office, I will arrest you. Understand?"

"I'm not an idiot."

He rolled his eyes. Clearly, he didn't agree with that statement. The nasty finger point only confirmed it.

"I'll be back in thirty seconds. Do. Not. Move."

She waved him away. "Yes, master."

The minute he left her office, Penny scooped up her purse, her cell phone and the phone Jenna had given her. At the door, she checked the hallway. Nothing. She ran to her father's office, fumbling through her office key ring as she went. After unlocking the door, she slipped in, grabbed his car keys from the desk drawer where he always kept them and said a silent thanks that he'd been escorted home and had left his car. For safety, she grabbed a folder out of his drawer. If Brent came back, she'd ditch her purse and say she needed the folder.

Hopefully, Brent needed a bowel movement that would buy her a few extra minutes. And what kind of insanity made her conjure that thought?

Forget it. Keep moving. She poked her head into the hallway. No Brent. All she needed to do was take a quick right, shortcut it through the conference room, exit the door on the other side and hit the emergency stairwell. With any luck, no one would see her.

Not that luck had been her friend recently. Not at all. And what was with these crazy thoughts? Her mind was a mess. *Keep moving.* She darted through the conference room, cracked the far door and peeked out. No life in the opposite hallway. *Perfecto.* She might pull this off. Once inside the stairwell, she kicked off her heels and bolted.

One way or another, she'd make this deal.

Alone.

RUSS'S PHONE RANG. Damned thing. He intended to ignore it, but since Hennings was on hold waiting for Penny, he checked the screen. Brent.

"What is it?"

"She's in the wind," he hollered.

"Come again?"

"Penny. I lost her."

Fierce banging ravaged Russ's skull. *Brutal.* He closed his eyes while he contemplated the murderous venom about to be unleashed. "How the hell—"

"Hey, unless you wanted me to piss myself, I needed a break."

"She bolted while you were in the john?"

Hennings snapped his eyes to Russ. "What?"

If he weren't so furious with her, Russ would find the simplicity of her escape comical. Russ jerked his chin at

Hennings. "Your daughter has eluded a U.S. marshal. While he relieved himself."

"I checked the whole office," Brent said. "No one saw her. I think she went out the emergency exit."

"Her car isn't at the office. She must have grabbed a cab. Get someone to her place. Fast." He went back to Hennings. "Do you have any idea what she's up to? She could get herself killed."

Something flickered in his eyes and he averted his gaze. This guy was good, but not that good. Russ spotted that momentary realization that his daughter may have just made a critical error. "My car is at the office. She knows where I keep my keys."

A litany of swearwords filled Russ's mind. He visualized wrapping them in twine, setting them aside for later. *Concentrate.* He went back to Brent. "She probably boosted her father's car. Had she taken any calls?"

"Only client calls that I could tell."

"Did any of them sound like Heath? Was she acting squirrelly?"

"No."

"Let me call you back." He hung up, threw his phone on Hennings's desk and it clattered against the solid wood. *Go to work.* Slowly, he raised his gaze to Hennings.

"Here's the short of it. The minute she gets out of her car, Heath will kill her. Zac will probably already be dead. Elizabeth Brooks and her son, having reneged on her agreement with the U.S. government, will no longer be under protection and will probably also be murdered. There you have it. Two of your three children murdered. Not to mention the client. That's what I'd call a bad freaking day."

"What the hell are you talking about?"

"Penny. She's on her way to see Heath. She made a deal with him. She all but admitted it to me."

"She wouldn't have done that."

"Well, she did. That makes us both suckers for your

daughter. She ditched her only protection and we have no idea where she's going. If I can find her, I'll intercept and maybe save her life."

The man's throat bobbed. *Come on, pops. Get to where I need you.*

Hennings stared down at his desk for a few seconds, then raised his gaze to Russ. "What do you need from me?"

Excellent. "She never goes anywhere without her phone. I need you to call your service provider and get a location on that phone. I could get a warrant, but that takes time, and by then Penny could be floating in a lake. We have a lot of lakes in this area."

Hennings didn't just go white; the man nearly keeled over. "That's not necessary."

Not necessary? Say what? One of the twines on the bushel of swearwords snapped. What could be more important than locating Penny? "Sir—"

He grabbed the cordless on the desk and dialed. "We have tracking on all company phones. All I need is the password. Hold on."

Russ waited, hands on hips, his fingers twitching while Hennings made a call. *Hurry up. Hurry up.* Every second was one second more Penny had. By now, she could be out of the city. Way ahead of him.

Penny's father jotted notes, hung up and swiveled sideways to his laptop. No time for that. Russ pulled his phone and grabbed the notes.

"Hold it," Hennings said.

"Sorry, sir. No time. You want your daughter back, it's my way."

He punched the website into his phone, only messing up twice because his damned fingers were too big for the screen and—there it was, the welcome screen where he loaded the user name and password. Within seconds a miniature map popped up. He zoomed in on the blinking red arrow.

"She just got on I-94. Heading north. What's she driving?"

"Probably my car. Mercedes S550. Black."

Russ ran toward the door. "Thank you. I'll call you when I've got her."

Which, if the map was correct, might not be for a while. Rotten luck that he was south of her location while she headed north. She'd managed to be a good forty miles in the opposite direction.

When he caught up, he'd kill her. No doubt about it.

PENNY PRESSED THE GAS on her father's car. At any second, Colin Heath would be calling with additional instructions. As he'd said he would, he called the disposable cell phone at two-thirty and told her to head north to Wisconsin. Then he'd hung up.

Which terrified her on several levels. The first being she was without any sort of backup, had no clue where she was headed and might walk into an ambush. For all she knew, Heath would kill her and Zac and then hunt down Elizabeth.

Call Russ. Penny checked the side mirror and switched lanes to avoid the slower car in front of her. *Outta the way, guy.* She despised fast driving, but in Chicago, if someone wasn't stuck in traffic, they'd better be keeping up. Or leading.

Worse, the sky had opened up and poured buckets of rain, making the road slick and turning sane drivers into lunatics. She cruised by the slower car and kept a good distance from the truck in front of her. *Hate trucks on an expressway.*

Not that she could avoid them, because she needed to get to the state line, where no one knew her whereabouts. At the very least, she should alert someone. If not Russ, then her father. Right? But he'd send someone to follow her, and Heath had warned her about that. *Come alone or Zac dies.*

She shook her head. These thoughts. Too much. Too many chances to make a fatal mistake.

Panic curled inside her, settled in her neck. She lifted one hand off the wheel and massaged the stiffness.

You need to do something. On the seat beside her, her work phone buzzed. She checked the screen. Russ. Again. He'd called at least five times. Chances were he'd keep calling. Time to face it. She clicked the speaker button and threw the phone back on the seat.

"Penny?"

And just the sound of his voice, that low resonance, even tinged with anger, brought a sense of order to her devoured mind.

She bit down on her bottom lip. *Don't lose it.* Inside her, all that emotion—fear, anxiety, heartbreak—sliced at her, ripping and tearing, stealing her air. *Can't breathe.* Tiny red dots swirled in front of her—truck lights—and she gripped the sweat-slicked wheel.

"Penny!"

Russ's hollering filled the car. *He's yelling at me.* Yelling? No, sir. She gasped and trapped air broke free, all that amazing oxygen clearing her fuzzy brain.

"Russell, I'm so sorry."

"Where are you?"

"On I-94."

"Where are you going?"

She couldn't tell him. Couldn't put everyone in danger. Even if it meant losing him, she couldn't risk it. She swatted at flowing tears. "I…I don't know. He hasn't told me yet. I'm so sorry. If I could have done it differently, I would. I hate that I've hurt you. I don't know how to fix this. I'm sorry. I adore you, Russell Voight. I just can't give you what you want. I need my brother back. And I need Elizabeth and Sam and you safe."

Flashing headlights in her rearview drew her attention. A car signaling her to get the heck out of the left lane. *Right. Pay attention.* Fearing blind spots that might cause a wreck and delay her, she swung a look over her shoulder and shifted lanes. *Focus. Concentrate on the road.*

"Listen to me," Russ said. "You're in over your head. We

can make this work. Together. If you haven't done anything yet, we can fix it. You need to pull over. Let me catch up and we'll work it out. We'll get Zac back and the you-and-me stuff, we'll figure it out. After the case is settled, we'll figure it out. If you get yourself killed, that's not helping anyone."

As if she didn't know that? "Russell, if I want my brother back alive, I need to do this. Alone."

Eyes still on the road, she fumbled over the phone's keypad and punched the button. Ridiculous man. Telling him where she was going would be the worst thing. Ever.

Phone. Her mind flashed to arguing with him the first time he'd confiscated her phone and taken the battery out.

"Oh, no. No. No. No."

She pulled to the shoulder and yanked the battery from her phone. "Stupid, Penny. Very stupid."

Chalk it up to stress killing her brain cells, because on a normal day, she'd have thought of that. At least she'd realized it before it was too late.

RUSS WATCHED THE RED ARROW disappear. "Oh, come on."

She'd turned the phone off. Probably pulled the battery, too. He'd wondered how long it would take her to figure it out. He shouldn't have called her. Critical error, that. But hey, this was what happened when law-enforcement people got emotional. They pushed too hard, got too dialed in to what they needed to close a case and tunnel vision set in. For him, falling for Penny was the final bullet into the heart of his case.

Not only had he lost complete control of a massive financial-fraud investigation, but by the time it all ended, he might have multiple homicides. Penny, Zac, Elizabeth and her son. Who knew?

He pressed the gas. At the time he spoke to her, she'd been twenty miles ahead of him on I-94 heading toward Wisconsin. He had twenty miles to figure something out.

Where the hell would she be heading?

He hasn't told me yet. That was what she'd said. Which meant she had an alternate way of communicating with Heath. And considering she was en route, it had to be a second cell phone.

Scanning his contacts while checking the road—total death wish—he found Brent's number and hit Speaker.

"You find her?" Brent huffed.

When they did find her, if Russ didn't kill her first, Brent would be there. This stunt had humiliated more than one federal agent.

"She's on I-94 but she just went dark. Which means she has a second phone."

"She always uses the office one."

"She's communicating with Heath somehow. Find that investigator she's using. Jenna someone. I'll explain later, but find her and ask her how Penny is communicating with Heath."

"I'm on it."

One thing about Brent, he understood urgency. Some guys would have wasted time peppering Russ with questions. Brent? He took action. Good man.

It took seven and a half minutes for Brent to call Russ back. And just in time because he was bearing down on the spot where he'd lost Penny.

"Got it," Brent said.

"What?"

"Jenna gave Penny one of her phones. It's a spare she keeps. She suspected Penny would go off the grid so she told her it was a disposable phone. It's not and when Penny left the office, Jenna tracked the phone. This chick is good. She's right behind her on I-94 and Penny doesn't know it."

The confined anger and hurt that had turned his body rock-hard unfurled into a flood of relief. His limbs and shoulders went loose and he breathed through it. "Jenna is aces. You got a number for her?"

"Yeah. Her cell."

"Text it to me and I'll call her."

"You got it. I'm jumping in my car now. Wherever Penny's going, we'll need backup."

"We gotta do it quietly. Penny is terrified, and if she knows we're behind her, she'll kill whatever this deal with Heath is. Nobody calls her. Let her think we don't know where she is."

"For how long?"

"Until we have Colin Heath either in handcuffs or a body bag."

IF PENNY'S LUCK had changed, she didn't know it. Not with the four-car pileup that had cars snarled on the highway, according to the local a.m. news report. Yep. Stopped dead in the middle lane, trapped by bumper-to-bumper vehicles, twenty miles from the Wisconsin border. No way to escape. A gurgle of hysterical laughter squeaked out and Penny slapped her hand over her mouth. As if that would keep her from completely losing whatever sanity she had left. Heath would be calling at any second, expecting her to be closer to the state line.

Well, he should be checking traffic, because she couldn't control horrid drivers. Even if the rain had stopped and the sun battled the afternoon clouds. All she wanted was her brother back. *Lie.* She didn't just want him back—she wanted him back alive. And unharmed.

If it took destroying the tentative beginnings of a relationship with Russ, she'd have to make that sacrifice. If he were half the man she hoped, he'd understand the impossible position she'd been faced with.

Still, in the back of her mind, she wondered if she should have clued Russ in earlier. Let him know what she was thinking. Maybe together, they could have figured out how to double-cross Heath.

Too late now. Her need to get Zac back twisted her mind,

sent her spiraling into a situation she failed to control. "So stupid, Penny."

She'd been too caught up in her emotions, not thinking clearly and had made a rash decision. Something completely out of character in her professional life. Her personal life was a different story, but never when it came to her clients.

On the seat beside her, the cell phone chirped. *Heath.* She scooped it up and hit the speaker button. "Hello?"

"Lovely Penny. What is your location?"

"I'm twenty miles from the border. Major traffic jam. We haven't budged in thirty minutes."

"Are you lying?"

How stupid would she be to lie about something like this? "Of course not. Check the traffic reports. I'm good, Heath, but I'm not good enough to airlift a car from bumper-to-bumper traffic."

"I see. When you cross into Wisconsin, pull into the first rest stop. Wait there for instructions."

"Where—"

Click. Dead air. "Hello?"

He'd hung up. She hurled the phone back onto the seat. "I've had enough of his nonsense."

And worse, she'd stolen her father's car. By now, he'd know and would be frantic. How much more could she put her family through? It had to stop. She slid a glance at the phone again. Contemplated calling her father. If she did, he'd have the number, and no doubt, Russ had already gone to him and convinced him Penny was in danger. That was all her father would hear and he'd cooperate. Whatever information the FBI needed to save his children, he'd offer.

No calls.

She was stuck. In traffic. With no idea where she was heading.

And she was alone.

How many smart-girl rules could she obliterate in one day? Apparently a lot. She slapped her hands over her face, took three deep breaths and let the last one out slowly. Her mind went quiet—better—and she slid her hands away to find the traffic ahead starting to move. Finally.

"I can do this. Heath wants this as much as I do."

Didn't he?

Chapter Eighteen

Russ drove into the rest stop where Brent had told him Penny parked. Visitors flowed in and out of the single-story brick building, some carrying food bags and drink cups, some rushing back to their cars. A young woman chased a toddler around the flagpole, and Russ watched for a second, hoping to hell Heath wasn't in this lot somewhere ready to open fire when he spotted Penny.

Not wanting to risk Penny seeing him, even if he had switched to another FBI undercover car and was on the other side of the busy lot, he nabbed the first available spot and scooted low in his seat while dialing Jenna.

"What's up?" Jenna asked.

"Do we have any idea where she's going?"

"No. She hasn't called me. Should I call her?"

Not in this lifetime, she shouldn't. Calling would only arouse Penny's suspicion. Then again, if she were communicating with Heath via the cell Jenna would call, chances were she wouldn't pull the battery on it. Couldn't risk it. "No. Let's just stay on her."

Stay on her he did. Twenty minutes after Russ had parked, Penny cruised her father's fancy Mercedes out of the rest stop and back onto the highway.

"Where the hell is she going?" he muttered.

His guess was rural. Nothing too urban. Rural gave more

opportunities to stay out of sight of law enforcement. Also made it easier to spot a tail. Like Russ.

And Brent.

And Jenna.

A flipping convoy. Not to mention the Milwaukee FBI field office that had been put on alert. This had to be his worst-nightmare scenario. Flying blind into a situation where he didn't know what kind of layout they'd face, how much firepower they'd be up against, and Penny, a woman he'd known he shouldn't get emotional about, would be in the middle of it.

Way to destroy a case.

If he walked away from this with a low body count, he'd have himself a minor miracle. But the media storm would be catastrophic. The headline would read "The Man Who Brought Down the Chicago Field Office."

Not the career notoriety he'd hoped for. *Do something.* Anything to figure out where Penny was heading. Right now, all he could do was follow her and hope he devised a plan before she wound up dead.

PENNY TOOK THE EXIT for Crowe, a town she'd never known existed. That wasn't saying much. Outside of the area where her parents owned their lake house, Wisconsin may as well have been a foreign country.

At the bottom of the exit ramp, she braked at the stop sign. Heath had told her to make a left and drive ten miles, at which point she'd receive her next set of instructions.

What she didn't like, aside from the entire godforsaken episode, was how incredibly rural this area was. To her left, the highway's bridge spanned a two-lane road. Beyond the bridge was a gas station circa 1949. She swung her head right. Cornfields. Miles and miles of cornfields. No trees as far as she could see. No cars or people, either.

How about a horse or even a damn rabbit? *Can I at least get an animal?* Some form of life?

Nothing.

The barren road and lack of activity made her itch, made the fact that she was alone in an unfamiliar area all too real.

This is wrong. All wrong.

And suddenly, the stress of the past few days brought the situation into sharp focus. Her terror over losing Zac had convinced her that allowing Heath to remain in control was the correct choice and she'd literally come to a crossroad. Now she needed to decide whether she'd call for help or drive straight into what might be the end of her life. Why should Heath let her or Zac live? Yes, she had evidence and maybe she could save herself by using that evidence as leverage, but Zac? He could easily become collateral damage.

She gripped the steering wheel, stared straight ahead at the adjacent ramp leading to the highway and knew she'd botched this.

Royally.

Assuming Heath might be watching from some hidden location, she turned left onto the rural road. In her cup holder sat her cell phone, not the one Jenna had given her, but her own.

The gas station loomed to her immediate right and she glanced at the gas dial. Half a tank. If she stopped, it would buy her time to shove the battery back into her phone. Someone, hopefully Russ, would then be able to locate her.

Without a doubt, at this moment, she needed Russ. He'd know what to do. As furious as he'd be with her, he wanted Heath and she could deliver. In the process, they needed to save Zac and give Elizabeth and her son their lives back.

Penny shook her head. These thoughts. Too much.

She drove into the gas station, where an attendant glanced out the window of the mini-mart. Grabbing her credit card from her purse, she got the pump started and jumped back into the car, where she dug out her phone's battery. She held it, wrapped her sweaty hand around it and squeezed.

It had to be the right thing. She glanced back at the pump.

Two gallons so far. Slow pump. If ever there was a sign, that had to be it. Keeping her arms low and out of sight, she slid the battery into her phone, stared at the black screen and ran her index finger along its smooth surface.

Russ would help her. He had to. She checked the pump. Five gallons. No more time to spare. Leaving the phone in the cup holder, she finished with the pump, settled back in the car and pulled onto the road while pressing the power button on her phone.

RUSS'S PHONE BEEPED just as he hit the exit ramp where Penny had gotten off the highway. Realizing how quiet the exit was, Brent had driven past and immediately alerted Russ that Penny had left the roadway, which he'd already known because Jenna was monitoring Penny's location from her own phone. All in all, this screwy team worked well together.

The phone beeped a second time and he checked the screen.

Penny Hennings.

A roaring blood surge left his arms and fingers and neck tingling. He hit the button just as he came to a stop at the bottom of the exit ramp.

"Penny?"

"Russell," she said. "I'm so sorry. Please. I don't know what to do. I thought I knew, but I don't and I've messed this whole thing up. It's all my fault. Heath threatened everyone. Zac, Elizabeth. You. Everyone I care about. I thought I could fix it."

Words flew at him—*my fault...Heath threatened...fix it*—and he took it all in until the stream finally stopped. "Penny?"

Another brief silence led to a sharp breath. "Please, Russell. I know you hate me."

"I don't hate you. You're too far inside your own head and you're not thinking straight. I'm pissed, but I don't hate you."

"I'm so sorry."

As mad as he was, he needed Killer Cupcake back on point. "This isn't your fault. As much as you want to believe that, it's not. Stop thinking it and concentrate. Where are you going?"

"I don't know. Heath keeps sending me to checkpoints and then he calls with instructions. I'm in Wisconsin."

"I know."

"You do?"

"The phone Jenna gave you, it's one of hers. We've been tracking you."

"Huh," Penny said, sounding fairly irritated.

Maybe later he'd laugh about that. Maybe. "I'm at the bottom of the exit ramp you just left."

"You *are?*"

"I don't know where the hell we're going, but I wasn't about to let you do this alone."

"Heath told me to make the left at the ramp and drive ten miles. I think he must be watching."

That, Russ was sure of. "I'm staying back. Just keep the phone line open so I can hear everything, okay? You must be getting close to wherever we're going. Once you know, we'll figure out a way out of this."

"Thank you."

"Don't thank me yet. We're not nearly done."

PENNY GLANCED DOWN at the car's odometer. Nine miles. One to go. In the next few minutes she'd be receiving another set of instructions. Typically, those instructions came by phone and there'd been no indication that would change.

She eased up on the gas pedal as the trees on the right side of the car cleared and the road dipped to a harsh, sloping hill. From her vantage point, she couldn't see beyond the slope, but a steel rail guarded the shoulder. From the battered look of it, more than a couple of cars had sideswiped it.

The blaring ring of Jenna's pseudodisposable phone filled

the silent car, the sound causing Penny to flinch. Yeesh. She snatched the phone, hit the speaker button and pulled to the side of the road before her nerves sent her careening into the much-visited guardrail.

"Hello?"

"Lovely Penny. Look to your right. See the quarry?"

Quarry. Okay, then. "Yes."

"Follow the road for one mile and turn right. Keep driving until you see the green shack of an office. I'm watching."

The line went silent.

Hung up. Again. Before she spoke, Penny pressed the end button, then did it again to make double-sure the call had disconnected.

"Russell?"

"I'm here," he said from his end of the other phone.

Penny held her hand over her lips in case anyone watched and could see her talking. "He's sending me into the quarry."

"I heard. I see it on the GPS. We've got backup and I'll have Brent get us a dump truck or something. We'll drive right in."

That'll be interesting. "Where is he getting a dump truck?"

Russ laughed. "Honey, he's a U.S. marshal. He'll go back to the highway, stop the first truck he sees and we have a truck."

I love this man. He had a spine of steel. Absolutely no challenge was too big to conquer. "Right. Good idea. What do I do?"

"Follow your instructions. We're here for you. You won't see us, and hopefully they won't, either, but we're here."

Just ahead, off to the right, a large sign with a giant red arrow pointed into what had to be the access road to the quarry. As she neared, the washed-out blue letters on the sign read Branley Stone.

Branley. Could be a town name. Or perhaps the owner's. She might never know.

"I'm turning in."

"I'm here."

I know. "Russell?"

"Yep."

"I love you."

Russ went quiet. They'd yet to talk about the first time she'd told him she loved him. Somehow she didn't mind. Or maybe she was afraid of what his reaction would be when they finally did discuss it. After what she'd done, he'd never trust her again.

"Penny," he finally said, and a small spark of hope lifted her mood, "you need to focus."

So much for hope. "I know."

"We'll talk about us later."

Fool. Had she expected him to return the sentiment? If Russ was the smart man she knew him to be, he'd run fast and far from the craziness known as Penny Hennings.

"Penny!"

She lurched. "Don't yell at me, *Russell.*"

"Then pay attention."

She came to the open quarry gate and drove through. A single-lane road had been blown out of the quarry walls and dipped right. She slid a glance sideways to the drop-off that led to a half-mile-wide and five-hundred-foot-deep hole in the earth. She clutched the steering wheel, holding it steady while she navigated the road that lined and lined and lined the outer rim of the quarry. Before she reached the bottom, where several trucks, tractors and odd pieces of equipment were scattered, she'd circle the entire thing. A shaft of sunlight broke through the clouds and blinded her. She squinted—*stop the car*—and pressed the brake, jerking the car to a stop. *Breathe.* She peered into the pit below, where the sun bounced off the steel roof of a rectangular building.

She'd have to battle the blinding sun the entire way. And pray she didn't nosedive off the road.

"You okay?" Russ asked.

"I'm adjusting to the sunlight. The green building is in the far corner toward the back."

"I know. We have agents up on the northeast bluff. They've got you. I'm coming around the back entrance."

"Thank you. Be careful of the road. It's so narrow, I'm afraid I'll roll off the side."

"You won't. There's nothing you can't handle. You're a hassle that way. You never give up."

Penny smiled, felt the rush of Lawyer Penny's return. "Oh, Russell. You're too good to me."

"I know. Now let's get your brother."

RUSS DROVE PAST the back entrance to the quarry. Heath had to have someone guarding the rear entrance. But what Russ banked on was the intel from the agents on the bluff that told him a thousand yards past the entrance was a field he could cut across to reach the road beyond the back entrance.

If Russ needed anything, he needed those agents to be right. He stormed down the country road, sun shining all around, and spotted a house a quarter mile down. Zac might be in that house. Might not.

Quarry.

Down deep, where his instincts guided the hard decisions, he knew Zac was in that quarry. To his left, a grassy field bumped against the perimeter of his target location and Russ swung into the field. As much as he wanted to hit the gas, he backed off as his bureau car bounced and thumped along the rutty ground.

When the field flattened out, he pressed the accelerator and the quarry came into view. Two minutes and he'd be there. He glanced to his left, but the rear entrance gate—and the man guarding it—couldn't be seen. If Russ couldn't see him, he couldn't see Russ.

The quarry walls and narrow road came into view. Killer

Cupcake wasn't kidding about that road. Russ hit the brakes and surveyed the area.

Damn it. The pit ahead was big and open, with only that one narrow strip of road circling it. If he continued on, he'd be burned. From his current spot, high on the bluff, he wouldn't be seen from below.

Cooked.

He dialed Brent, who answered after two rings. "What's up?"

"I'm in. Up on the southeast bluff. Can't go anywhere, though, or I'll be burned. No place to hide once I hit the road."

"Can you see her?"

"No. What's your status?"

"I got you a truck. The driver is not too happy. We're seven minutes out. Give or take."

Nice. Russ bumped his fist against the steering wheel. Finally a break.

"Okay. Call me when you're here. Once we get confirmation on Zac, we'll drive right in like we're here on business."

"Hey, we're not bringing the driver in there. No way. Can you drive this thing?"

I think so. "I used to drive a flatbed tow truck for the garage where my dad worked. I'll figure it out."

"You sure?"

"I have to be. We can't leave her down there alone."

PENNY PARKED BESIDE the office and turned off the engine. *Here we go.* She studied the layout of the dilapidated building. Small porch. Not even a chair would fit. Two windows to the left of the door. One to the right. That one was cracked and had a closed sign in front of the shade. *They all have shades.* No sign of a rifle barrel anywhere. That was good because, at the moment, she made an easy target. She looked up. No one on the roof.

These thoughts. What nonsense. If they intended to kill her, she'd be dead already. The goon she'd spotted standing at the rear of the building when she'd parked was enough of an indication of that.

Just ahead, the freshly painted steps were the only part of this dump that looked sturdy. The dwelling couldn't have been more than three rooms. Could be good. Could be bad.

The door opened and Penny stopped two feet before reaching the steps. *If they wanted to kill me, they'd have done it already.* She focused on that thought, let it take root, let it bring alive the in-command-lawyer part of her rather than the terrified victim. Lawyer Penny could handle this.

She breathed in, watched as a tall man with dark hair stepped into view. He wore jeans and a loose T-shirt. Thin build.

Heath.

"Lovely Penny," he said in that annoying soft voice he probably thought was charming. "Welcome. Please, come in."

"Where's Zac?"

Heath swung sideways, waved her in. "He's in here."

Penny stayed put. If she stepped into that office, he'd likely shut the door behind her and she and Zac would both be trapped. If Zac was even in there.

"Zac?" she hollered.

"I'm here" came the immediate reply.

Her brother's voice, strong and direct, just as he sounded in court. If he were in pain, she'd hear it. Or sense it. Something. A rush of relief shot up her back, somehow lifted her higher, strengthened her. *He's alive.*

"Let's do this outside," she told Heath.

"No."

Again with controlling the environment. Heath always

managed the upper hand. That had to stop. But now, with Zac inside, she wasn't sure what choice she had. Plus, Russ was here. With backup. Watching and waiting.

Penny stepped forward, climbed the stairs and entered the office. A blast of frigid air surrounded her as the ancient air conditioner above her head cranked and whined. When she breathed in, the unmistakable intake of dust traveled down her throat. On her left was a desk piled high with papers. Down the short hallway, she saw a second metal desk and beside it sat Zac, his big body consuming the narrow chair.

She charged toward him, wobbling on the stupid stilt shoes as she ran. Zac's wrists were zip-tied, the plastic cutting into his skin, leaving his flesh pink and swollen on the sides. He brought his bound hands up just as she entered the tiny room, and the barrel of a rifle swung into view.

"Stay back," Zac said.

She turned toward the weapon being held by one of Heath's flunkies, an average-size guy with light brown hair and a long, narrow face, standing in the corner. Could he be the courthouse shooter? The man grinned at her—vile man—and she turned back to Zac.

"Are you okay?"

He nodded, and despite his wrinkled shirt and *missing jacket,* not to mention the mussed hair, he appeared unharmed.

She faced Heath. "Here's the deal. When I take him out of here, Elizabeth disappears. No testifying. I keep any evidence she has. Call it my safety net. If anything happens to her or anyone I care about, I turn that evidence over to the FBI."

"Or I could kill you both right here."

He could. "But you won't because you don't know where that evidence is. Elizabeth will still disappear and you'll wonder what safeguards I've established. I can tell you, if I don't walk out of here with my brother, you're going to prison. Bet on it."

RUSS, BRENT AND a highly agitated thirtysomething truck driver stood on an obscure dirt road a mile from the quarry while Russ stared up at the giant 18-wheeler Brent had commandeered.

An 18-wheeler. Not only had it been ten years since he'd driven a truck, he'd never attempted anything this size. But hey, now would be as good a time as any.

"Seriously, dude," the truck driver said. "I got a load that needs to be delivered by six. My boss will kill me."

Russ ditched his tie and started unbuttoning his dress shirt. "No, he won't. You'll stay here. I'm driving. The FBI will take responsibility."

Sure they will. Russ Voight, the man who brought down the Chicago field office.

He stripped down to his undershirt and tossed the dress shirt into his car. When he drove into the quarry, anyone who spotted him would see a man in a white T-shirt rather than clothing that screamed FBI.

"I'm going with you," Brent said.

"Uh, no. It'll look suspicious if there are two."

"You're not going in alone. Besides, she's my responsibility."

Russ glanced up, saw the set jaw and knew Brent wouldn't cave. This was a matter of pride. Penny had been under his protection and he'd lost her—a macho-code violation for sure. Russ would feel the same way.

"Fine. But you squat on the floor."

"What's the plan?"

"Hell if I know. We're driving in and drawing them out of that office. He's got men watching. A truck entering will rattle them, but it's not totally out of the realm of reason."

"And once we get in there?"

"No clue."

Brent huffed, "Great."

"Hey, I'm open to ideas, but until we get there, we don't know. There's men on the north and southeast bluffs. They've got us." Russ turned to the truck driver. "You stay here."

The guy nodded.

Good enough. "Let's roll."

Chapter Nineteen

"We got a problem," someone barked through Heath's radio.

Penny stood still, no twitching fingers, no scrunching her nose, no tapping foot, nothing that would indicate any form of a reaction.

Heath ripped the radio from his belt and hit the button. "What?"

"There's a truck coming through the gate."

Russ.

Heath swung to the ape with the rifle. "What the hell is this, now?"

The guy shrugged. "I'll check it out."

"There's nothing on the schedule." He jerked his chin toward Zac and Penny. "We'll lock them in here and both go."

Yes, please. Lock us in. It would give them a second to form some kind of a plan as Russ drove whatever truck they'd confiscated down that treacherous entry road.

And heaven help him if he couldn't control that thing, because he'd tumble off the side of the quarry. She held her breath a second, refusing to show any emotion until Heath and his goon left.

When the lock snicked from the outer hallway, she spun to Zac, bent low next to his ear. "It's Russ driving that truck."

Zac nodded. "Check the desk. See if there's a scissors or something to cut these zip ties. We need to get outta here."

"How?"

He gestured to the wall and the door with a full glass panel in the middle. "Through there. It's locked, but we can break the glass."

Penny turned to the glass door and her stomach clenched. Her brother was suddenly delusional. Still, she raced to the desk, rifled through the thin drawer on the underside of the desk. No scissors. Quickly, she checked the side drawers. "How are we getting through the glass?"

"It's a cheap door. Get my hands free and I'll toss the chair through it. Hurry up, Pen."

She closed the last drawer and checked under the files on top of the desk. "There's nothing here."

"Forget it. I'll work around the ties."

"How?"

Zac twisted his hands and clamped each one clawlike around the top rung of the chair. "Like that. Back up."

Using little effort, he swung the chair once, then a second time to get some momentum.

"Zac, be..."

Crash. The chair sailed through the glass that rained down in varying chunks and shards and landed with a tinkling sound all around.

"Careful."

"Go, Pen!"

She grabbed his arm and the two of them leaped through the open frame to the small porch. Her left foot wobbled—stupid shoes—and her ankle gave way. She stumbled as her ankle collapsed and a piercing pain shot up her calf. "Ow."

"Are you hurt?"

"Twisted my ankle. Damned heels."

Ditch the shoes. She kicked her shoes off, felt a stab of glass on the ball of her foot—*worry about it later*—and ran toward Dad's car. Zac ran beside her, clearly not willing to pass her despite his much longer legs being able to make it happen. Her brother never left her stranded. Never.

From the opposite side of the office, Heath rounded the corner, a pistol in his hand. He halted and aimed the gun at Penny, tracking her movements as she ran. *No, no, no.*

"Stop," Heath said, his voice low and calm and cutting. "Or I kill her right here."

Madman. "Go, Zachary. He won't do it."

"Yeah, I will. At this point, my options are dwindling. If killing you both means getting out of here, I'll do it."

"The trucker," Penny said.

"Another body won't matter."

"STAY DOWN," RUSS muttered to Brent, who had squeezed his giant body into the passenger-side floorboard.

"Roger that."

Russ hit the brake, jerking the big rig as he maneuvered down the treacherous road. If he hit a hole the wrong way, the truck could drop into the pit.

"Don't kill us," Brent said.

Russ grunted. Brent would pay for that later. He hit the gas and focused on the road ahead. Almost there.

Movement to the left of the office drew his gaze. "What the hell?"

"What?"

"A chair just flew through a window. Or maybe a door. Can't tell. Oh, crap. Zac jumped out. With Penny."

Get there. Russ pressed the accelerator, shifting fast. Grinding the gear wasn't stellar—*damn*—but the big tires dug in, sending the truck roaring forward. Another sixty yards and they'd hit the bottom of the road and have a flat surface straight to Penny and Zac.

Two men tore around the building. One appeared to be Heath, but from this distance, Russ couldn't be sure. One man carried a rifle, the other a handgun. The one with the handgun stopped, brought the gun up toward Penny's and Zac's chests. Russ banged on the steering wheel, trying to breathe, but nothing. *Damn it, damn it, damn it.*

He'd watch her tiny body drop, that blond hair flying and blood seeping from her as she went down. She'd die in front of him and he couldn't breathe, couldn't help her, couldn't stop it. *I never said it.* Never told her he loved her. She'd die and he'd never said it.

In front of him, Penny kept running. As usual, pressing on, because that was what Killer Cupcake did. She never gave up. Suddenly, Russ's chest unlocked and a burst of oxygen shot into his lungs.

"Go!" he hollered as if she could hear him.

Penny ran toward her father's Mercedes and the second guy, the one with the rifle, aimed right at her. *Stop him.*

Russ sat on the truck's horn, the sound filling his head, slamming around. The unsub spun to the truck, fired off a round. Russ flinched and the blast shattered the truck's windshield, sending shards of glass flying. He reared back, thankful for the sunglasses protecting his eyes, and ripped his Glock from his waist holster.

"Damn it!" Brent hollered, scrambling up from the floorboard.

"He's at two o'clock," Russ said. "Two o'clock."

The truck bounced and Russ held the wheel steady. *Aim low.* If he aimed low, when the truck moved upward, the shot would come up to meet his target. Wait for it. Now. *Boom, boom, boom*—three shots—dead ahead.

Missed.

Brent fired three rounds. Another loud boom sounded from the bluff and the target dropped, his body crumpling to the ground. *Someone got him.*

With Brent offering cover, Russ set his Glock in his lap to shift and swung the truck toward the two men chasing Penny and Zac. He blasted the horn again, the truck's engine roaring as the guy chasing Penny—presumably Heath—body-slammed her into the Mercedes.

Now I'm pissed. Every moment spent pursuing this animal funneled into a series of hot stabs carving him right down the middle. A vision of shoving Heath into a cell, a cold, filthy cell, and mashing his face into the wall, letting him get a taste of the misery, popped into Russ's mind. He'd find him the worst prison he could. No country clubs.

He slammed the truck to a stop. "You've got Zac," he said as he jumped from the cab.

"On it." Brent charged to the second guy, who'd tackled Zac and was still on the ground.

Heath glanced back, spotted Russ and—*yow*—hauled Penny up by her hair, swung her around and held her in front of him, the barrel of his gun shoved at her neck.

Russ slid a glance right. Brent. Gun. Second guy down. Weapon secured. *Cuff him.*

It's me and Heath now. And the agents on the bluff. But Penny was too close. If they took a shot and missed, they'd kill her. Still, with her small size, Heath had a good ten inches on her.

Make this shot.

Penny stood in front of Heath, her cheeks hollowed, jaw set, eyes focused on him. And if he knew her at all, thinking about how to get herself out of this mess.

Russ raised his Glock, trained it on Heath's head. Penny's gaze shot left, right and down. "Russ?"

"Shut up!" Heath hollered.

And if Russ wasn't mistaken, Heath's gun hand quivered. Add to that the sweat pouring down his face and his damp hair and the guy had a mountain of stress indicators. *Nervous.*

Nervous men got amped-up trigger fingers.

He checked on Penny and her gaze drifted down again. Definitely a message.

"Let her go, Heath. This is over. You're leaving here in a body bag or cuffs. Your choice."

Heath yanked on Penny's hair again—one wicked thrust—and her eyes flew open. She made a hissing sound and Russ checked his gun sights again. *Just give me the shot.*

From the corner of his eye, he spotted Brent rolling the other guy to his belly and cuffing his hands behind his back. The big marshal stood tall and pointed at Zac, who also still had his hands zip-tied.

"Sit on him if you have to, but make sure he doesn't move," Brent told Zac.

Wasting no time, Zac marched over and did as he was told.

Brent turned his sidearm on Heath, who angled Penny so he could see Russ and Brent. "Nobody moves!"

Again Penny looked down, then came back to Russ. "Russ?"

"You're okay," he said. "I've got this."

She brought her foot up and—*oofff*—slammed her bare heel into Heath's shin. *Nice.* The woman was fierce. Her kick slid away, but Heath bucked, gave Penny a second to shift right, far enough where Russ could get a shot off and not hit her. All movement slowed, the air became still, voices muffled as Penny swung an elbow and Russ focused on his target, focused on that spot on his forehead that would send him lights out. *Penny's too close.* He shifted to his right—*gotta aim right*—and *crack*. The sound of the shot echoed through the quarry. *Focus, focus, focus.* The bullet connected just above Heath's left eye, he stumbled back, his eyes rolling. Down he went.

Brent charged in, sidearm drawn, while Russ gave cover. Penny stood to the side, her face white, eyes flat and dead as she took in the chaos. "You're okay," he said, refusing to go to her until Brent had given him the go sign. The marshal reached Heath, bent low, checked his pulse.

"We're clear," he said.

Dead. For the first time in Russ's career, he'd killed a man. Later, he'd figure out what to do with the emotions involved in that. Later…

He turned to Zac, still literally sitting on their suspect. "You good?"

"Yeah," he said. "Take care of Penny."

Sirens blared from the top of the pit, the sound drawing closer as the seconds ticked by. The other agents would help clear the area, make sure they'd gotten all the unsubs. No runners. Not this time. Russ wanted them all.

Penny remained in her spot, still with the stoic eyes staring down at Heath's dead body. He'd terrorized her. Put fear into her. And now he was a bloody stump.

"Penny?" Russ said, finally drawing her attention.

"He's dead?"

"He is."

Russ glanced at her feet, where blood drops dotted the ground. He rushed over. Grabbed her arm and squeezed. "You're bleeding."

"It's glass. From the door. I kicked off my shoes to..."

To run. She shook her head and that capped it. Ignoring the fact that Brent watched, Russ wrapped his arms around her, held her and breathed, because he'd never been so terrified of losing someone. She squeezed him tight and a chunk of that fear broke away. "You're okay, right?"

"I'm fine. Just my feet."

"I'm sorry."

She dropped her head against his shoulder. Resting.

"Thank you, Russ."

He ran his free hand over the back of her head and laughed. "That's twice now you've called me Russ."

He stepped back, smiled down at her. "I got you to call me Russ." He turned to the man—the extremely dead man—that had consumed him for over a year. *It's over.* He'd wanted his case closed, but wasn't yet sure how he felt about this ending.

Having Penny next to him was what mattered. That, he knew. Maybe this was what taking a life did to people. Made them think too hard about too many things.

Around them, cars and vans and BearCats screamed to a stop, and men dressed in tactical gear swarmed. Zac was relieved of his post, his prisoner brought to a squad car while Brent tended to freeing Zac's hands. Pulling Penny closer, Russ kissed the top of her head, breathed in the scent of her shampoo, and something flicked inside him. Fear releasing. Whatever it was, he didn't care. She was alive. "Go see your brother. We'll talk later."

Chapter Twenty

Using the code Russ had recited over the phone, Penny opened his garage door. She took that as a good sign for their big talk. After all, if a man wanted to dump someone, he wouldn't part with his garage code. Plus, she'd floated the trial balloon of bringing dinner and he'd agreed. Garage code plus dinner, in Penny's mind, equaled hope.

Adding to the positive vibe was the fact that he lived minutes from her parents. In a two-story Colonial. Russell Voight, suburbanite. Who knew? The door slid up and revealed his bureau car parked on the right of the two-car garage.

Carrying two grocery bags with the fixings for dinner, she strode to the entry door, where a mudroom—an incredibly organized mudroom with a built-in wall unit—greeted her. Russ was an organized man. Another plus in a long list of pluses.

She moved through the mudroom to a roomy kitchen where guests could easily gather. Maybe the counters looked a little sparse and the farm table needed a centerpiece, but the area was tidy and the scent of lemons hung in the air. Which led Penny to believe one thing: Russ had a cleaning lady.

Oh, this man. Organized and a dedication to cleanliness. *I will love him fiercely.* If he'd let her. And when had she become a woman who waited for a man to *let* her do anything? She didn't know. Didn't necessarily believe it, either, because she'd walked away from plenty of men in her life. Plenty.

With Russ, she didn't mind that there were times—like now—she'd be willing to take a chance on him demolishing her heart. Maybe, with the right man, a man who wouldn't use vulnerability as a weapon against her, it wasn't a bad thing.

For once, she cared enough to allow herself to be vulnerable. To fight for him. To be humbled.

To a point, she'd suck it up. If he booted her, that would be it. She wouldn't beg. Not ever. She'd simply stab him and leave.

Good plan, Penny.

In the kitchen, the sliding glass door led to a cement patio and—look at that—a swimming pool. She'd fallen in love with this man despite not knowing he lived in the suburbs in a wildy traditional house with an inground pool. Hopefully, she'd continue to learn interesting things about him.

She set the bags on the counter, slid the door open and stepped into the yard, where Bruce Springsteen's voice drifted from speakers at the corners of the patio.

Russ sat in a floating lounge chair, his head back, eyes closed and a can of pop drooping precariously in his hand. He wore blue swim trunks with white trim and his skin and hair dripped with water. *Just took a swim.* He looked... peaceful. Instantly, as if it had reached out and wrapped itself around her, that peace melted into her and made her normally hyperefficient body loosen.

"Special Agent Voight, are you sleeping?"

He lifted his head and a slow smile spread his lips. "Barely."

"Good. How was your day?"

Last night, as part of the investigation into Heath's death, Russ had immediately been given time off. Procedure, he'd assured her, seeming unconcerned about the incident being cleared. After the destruction Heath had caused, she couldn't imagine Russ suffering repercussions for his actions.

"I've had an exciting day of floating," he said, light on the sarcasm.

Like her, he wanted to be part of the action. She'd probably be irritated, too. "Did you hear from your office?"

"My supervisor called. They scored big-time at Heath's office. He's been running scams all over the country with at least twenty-five other people in on it. They're all in custody. And the guy we took out at the quarry? He was Randy Jones's brother."

Penny closed her eyes, let the feeling of total relief overtake her. *It's over.* They'd confirmed the man as the courthouse shooter. Now Elizabeth and Sam could get on with their lives. Penny opened her eyes again. "You promised me you'd get him and you did. Thank you."

He shrugged. "Team effort. Sorry about your assistant."

"Yeah. That was a shocker. Poor thing is devastated over putting us in danger. She had no idea who Heath was, but technically, she broke privilege by sharing firm information. It's an ethics violation. Now we have to decide what to do with her."

"Can you trust her?"

"That's the million-dollar question. My father wants to fire her. And he has every right to. He told me to sleep on it and we'll discuss it in the morning. I feel bad for her. She got duped by the guy, but I can't get beyond what she did. I think she has to go. What kind of message does it send if we keep her?"

"That it's okay to talk about clients to nonemployees. You can't have that."

"Exactly." She shook her head. "I'll figure it out."

Russ pointed at her feet. "Do they hurt?"

She looked down at her flat shoes. With the condition of her feet, she might never wear heels again. "They're okay. The glass is out."

"Why don't you ditch those clothes and jump in here with me?" He waggled his eyebrows. "I'll help you forget the pain."

Another good sign. "I didn't bring a suit."

"You need a suit?"

At that, she laughed. "Russell!"

He whirled his index finger. "Privacy fences. The neighbors can't see."

She glanced to either side. A red ranch sat on one side and a two-story home on the other, but that one was angled away from Russ's yard, so only the side of the house was visible. The side with no windows. She turned back to him. "You devil. Besides, we're supposed to have our talk."

"We are talking. Now help me christen this pool. I've never had a naked woman in here."

Did she really need to hear that? "TMI, *Russell.* TMI. How long have you lived here?"

"Six months."

"The pool was here?"

"Yep. When I was a kid I always wanted a pool. I guess you could say the house came with the pool. I want you to be the first—and only—woman who gets naked with me in here."

Such a pig. "I have to put dinner together."

He grinned. "You're cooking?"

"Of course."

"You said you'd bring dinner. You didn't say you were cooking? Killer Cupcake cooks?"

"*Killer Cupcake?* What the hell?"

Russ laughed. "Forget it. Come in here with me. We'll float around. Relax a little. You do relax, don't you?"

Not usually. But suddenly, relaxing seemed like a great idea. Particularly with him.

"I have to say, I'm a bit shocked you live in the suburbs. I pictured you living downtown."

"Okay," he said. "I'll play. I like the burbs. It's quiet. I don't get a lot of quiet in my line of work. With the quiet, I like to float in my pool. A pool I want you to be in—naked—with me because, crazy as this might sound, I'm nuts about a smart-mouthed, high-strung defense attorney who probably won't give me a second of peace."

"I'm high-strung?"

"After that speech, you're latching on to high-strung? And, please. You know you're high-strung. But so am I. Sometimes. I think it'll work. I think *we'll* work. But I'm not saying that because I want you naked—although we have established that's my goal here."

Penny cracked up and he smiled a lightning-quick smile that told her he knew he was winning. A half-full water bottle sat on the edge of the pool. She picked it up, checked its weight and hurled it at him. It smacked him on his upper arm, splashed into the pool and floated next to him. He let it be.

"You're a pig, *Russell.*"

"I'm a man. We're all pigs."

She shook her head. Slowly gave in to the idea that before the night was through she'd be naked and in this pool. "Some truth to that. I take it by the whole getting-naked thing you're not dumping me?"

He paddled his way to the side of the pool. Finally, he'd relieve her of this misery.

She squatted down and he tugged on a strand of her hair that had fallen loose. "In the kitchen. Check the cabinet next to the slider. I left you something."

"What is it?"

"Will you just do what I say for once? Shut up and go look."

Penny stood tall, backed up a few steps in case Russ got playful and tried to splash her. "I'll be back."

In the kitchen, she opened the cabinet. The top shelf held canned goods. The second shelf a variety of boxed items and snacks. The bottom shelf, a shelf a person of her diminutive size could reach—*points for that, big boy*—was lined with jars and jars of…white gummy bears. *What did he do?* She slid one jar out. Behind it was another jar. And another. Three rows, five across, of white gummy bears.

She dropped her chin to her chest and let her head hang while her system adjusted to the weightlessness of the past days being gone. *This man.* So right for her. She grabbed one of the jars and squeezed it. He must have been separating gummy bears for hours.

For her.

"Did you find it?" Russ yelled.

Oh, I found it. She took the jar back to the side of the pool and squatted again. "How long did it take you?"

He shrugged. "I couldn't sleep. It happens after a big case. I get jumpy. The sorting settles my mind."

"You're amazing. Thank you."

"You're welcome." He grabbed on to the side of the pool to keep from floating away and held her gaze. "Look, it's early yet for us. I can't promise a lot. I'm stubborn as hell and I screw up sometimes. I'm not a romantic. I'll never remember to send you flowers on the anniversary of our first date. I won't snuggle when the Bears, the Sox *or* the Bulls are on, and you can bet I won't carry your purse under any circumstances. I'm not that guy. But I can promise that I'll take care of you. I will go to war for you when you need it, and I will love you inside and out. No question. Whatever happens, I know, *I know,* any mistakes you make are made out of passion and love. So, yeah, there will always be a jar of white gummy bears waiting in that cabinet for you. *That's* the guy I am. The one who knows what moves you."

He'd forgiven her. She'd nearly destroyed his case and he'd just forgiven her. *I will love him fiercely.* She reached out, ran her hand over the dark swirly hair on his chest. "Maybe I need *that* guy."

He glanced down at her hand, grabbed it and linked his fingers with hers. "I love you. I think I loved you that first day when you tore me up on the stand. A woman who could do that and still make me want her? I knew you were special."

He loved her. She leaned forward, kissed the back of his hand still joined with hers. For months they'd been circling each other and had finally figured it out. "I love you, too. Even if you don't like defense attorneys."

"Hey, I like one. And she's the important one."

Penny stood, left the gummy bears on the side of the pool and slid her unbuttoned suit jacket off. She tossed it on one of the lounge chairs. Russ watched her unbutton the sleeves of her blouse and a thousand small tingles zipped up her arms.

"You're coming in?"

"After the gummy bears? You bet I am."

Russ tilted his head. "What about dinner?"

"Are you starving?"

"Not for food."

Penny laughed and stripped off her shirt. "Special Agent Voight, you'd better not break my heart. I'd have to stab you if you did."

"Talk about romance."

"Just warning you."

Using one hand, he pushed himself away from the side of the pool, splashing a bit of water as he went. She took it all in, the man, the water, the quiet, and imagined him in ten years—twenty maybe—gray hair at his temples. Balding? How funny that would be. All that thick dark hair gone. She might like it. Either way, he'd be home. That place where she could be vulnerable and it wouldn't hurt or weaken her.

Slipping off the last of her clothing, she walked to the edge of the pool, felt his gaze on her as she went. "You're it for me, Penny. We'll get old together."

Yes, they would. At least, if they didn't kill each other first. "Count on it, Russ."

* * * * *

COMING NEXT MONTH FROM

HARLEQUIN®

INTRIGUE®

Available June 17, 2014

#1503 WEDDING AT CARDWELL RANCH

Cardwell Cousins • by B.J. Daniels

Someone is hell-bent on making Allie Taylor think she's losing her mind. Allie's past has stalked her to Cardwell Ranch, and not even Jackson Cardwell may be able to save her from a killer with a chilling agenda.

#1504 HARD RIDE TO DRY GULCH

Big "D" Dads: The Daltons • by Joanna Wayne

Faith Ashburn turns to sexy detective Travis Dalton to find and save her missing son. In the process, will Travis lose his heart and find a family?

#1505 UNDERCOVER WARRIOR

Copper Canyon • by Aimée Thurlo

Was Agent Kyle Goodluck's last undercover assignment too close to home for comfort? Now Kyle's only hope to prevent an attack that would rock the entire nation is the mysterious woman he's just rescued from terrorists, Erin Barrett.

#1506 EXPLOSIVE ENGAGEMENT

Shotgun Weddings • by Lisa Childs

Stacy Kozminski and Logan Payne must fake an engagement to survive. But with someone trying to kill them with bullets and bombs, they may never make it to the altar.

#1507 STRANDED

The Rescuers • by Alice Sharpe

When detective Alex Foster returns from the dead, he wants two things: his estranged, pregnant wife, Jessica, to love him, and to capture the man who wants them both dead....

#1508 SANCTUARY IN CHEF VOLEUR

The Delancey Dynasty • by Mallory Kane

Hannah Martin flees to New Orleans looking for help from PI Mack Griffin. It doesn't take him long to appreciate Hannah's courage and resourcefulness, or to realize that he may end up needing protection, too—from his feelings for her.

YOU CAN FIND MORE INFORMATION ON UPCOMING HARLEQUIN® TITLES, FREE EXCERPTS AND MORE AT WWW.HARLEQUIN.COM.

HICNM0614

REQUEST YOUR FREE BOOKS!
2 FREE NOVELS PLUS 2 FREE GIFTS!

HARLEQUIN®

INTRIGUE®

BREATHTAKING ROMANTIC SUSPENSE

YES! Please send me 2 FREE Harlequin Intrigue® novels and my 2 FREE gifts (gifts are worth about $10). After receiving them, if I don't wish to receive any more books, I can return the shipping statement marked "cancel." If I don't cancel, I will receive 6 brand-new novels every month and be billed just $4.74 per book in the U.S. or $5.24 per book in Canada. That's a savings of at least 14% off the cover price! It's quite a bargain! Shipping and handling is just 50¢ per book in the U.S. and 75¢ per book in Canada.* I understand that accepting the 2 free books and gifts places me under no obligation to buy anything. I can always return a shipment and cancel at any time. Even if I never buy another book, the two free books and gifts are mine to keep forever.

182/382 HDN F42N

Name (PLEASE PRINT)

Address Apt. #

City State/Prov. Zip/Postal Code

Signature (if under 18, a parent or guardian must sign)

Mail to the **Harlequin® Reader Service:**

IN U.S.A.: P.O. Box 1867, Buffalo, NY 14240-1867

IN CANADA: P.O. Box 609, Fort Erie, Ontario L2A 5X3

Are you a subscriber to Harlequin Intrigue books and want to receive the larger-print edition?

Call 1-800-873-8635 or visit www.ReaderService.com.

* Terms and prices subject to change without notice. Prices do not include applicable taxes. Sales tax applicable in N.Y. Canadian residents will be charged applicable taxes. Offer not valid in Quebec. This offer is limited to one order per household. Not valid for current subscribers to Harlequin Intrigue books. All orders subject to credit approval. Credit or debit balances in a customer's account(s) may be offset by any other outstanding balance owed by or to the customer. Please allow 4 to 6 weeks for delivery. Offer available while quantities last.

Your Privacy—The Harlequin® Reader Service is committed to protecting your privacy. Our Privacy Policy is available online at www.ReaderService.com or upon request from the Harlequin Reader Service.

We make a portion of our mailing list available to reputable third parties that offer products we believe may interest you. If you prefer that we not exchange your name with third parties, or if you wish to clarify or modify your communication preferences, please visit us at www.ReaderService.com/consumerschoice or write to us at Harlequin Reader Service Preference Service, P.O. Box 9062, Buffalo, NY 14269. Include your complete name and address.

HI13R

SPECIAL EXCERPT FROM

HARLEQUIN®

INTRIGUE®

Read on for a sneak peek of
WEDDING AT CARDWELL RANCH
by New York Times *bestselling author*

B.J. Daniels

Part of the ***CARDWELL COUSINS*** *series.*

In Montana for his brother's nuptials,
Jackson Cardwell isn't looking to be anybody's hero.
But the Texas single father knows a beautiful lady in
distress when he meets her.

"I'm afraid to ask what you just said to your horse," Jackson joked as he moved closer. Her horse had wandered over to some tall grass away from the others.

"Just thanking him for not bucking me off," she admitted shyly.

"Probably a good idea, but your horse is a she. A mare."

"Oh, hopefully she wasn't insulted." Allie actually smiled. The afternoon sun lit her face along with the smile.

He felt his heart do a loop-de-loop. He tried to rein it back in as he looked into her eyes. That tantalizing green was deep and dark, inviting, and yet he knew a man could drown in those eyes.

Suddenly, Allie's horse shied. In the next second it took off as if it had been shot from a cannon. To her credit, she hadn't let go of her reins, but she grabbed the saddle horn and let out a cry as the mare raced out of the meadow headed for the road.

Jackson spurred his horse and raced after her. He could hear the startled cries of the others behind him. He'd been riding since he was a boy, so he knew how to handle his horse. But Allie, he could see, was having trouble staying in the saddle with her horse at a full gallop.

He pushed his horse harder and managed to catch her, riding alongside until he could reach over and grab her reins. The horses lunged along for a moment. Next to him Allie started to fall. He grabbed for her, pulling her from her saddle and into his arms as he released her

HIEXP69770

reins and brought his own horse up short.

Allie slid down his horse to the ground. He dismounted and dropped beside her. "Are you all right?"

"I think so. What happened?"

He didn't know. One minute her horse was munching on grass, the next it had taken off like a shot.

Allie had no idea why the horse had reacted like that. She hated that she was the one who'd upset everyone.

"Are you sure you didn't spur your horse?" Natalie asked, still upset.

"She isn't wearing spurs," Ford pointed out.

"Maybe a bee stung your horse," Natalie suggested.

Dana felt bad. "I wanted your first horseback-riding experience to be a pleasant one," she lamented.

"It was. It is," Allie reassured her, although in truth, she wasn't looking forward to getting back on the horse. But she knew she had to for Natalie's sake. The kids had been scared enough as it was.

Dana had spread out the lunch on a large blanket with the kids all helping when Jackson rode up, trailing her horse. The mare looked calm now, but Allie wasn't sure she would ever trust it again.

Jackson met her gaze as he dismounted. Dana was already on her feet, heading for him. Allie left the kids to join them.

"What is it?" Dana asked, keeping her voice down.

Jackson looked to Allie as if he didn't want to say in front of her.

"Did I do something to the horse to make her do that?" she asked, fearing that she had.

His expression softened as he shook his head. "You didn't do *anything*." He looked at Dana. "Someone shot the mare."

Someone is hell-bent on making Allie Taylor think she's losing her mind. Jackson's determined to unmask the perp. Can he guard the widowed wedding planner and her little girl from a killer with a chilling agenda?

Find out what happens next in
WEDDING AT CARDWELL RANCH
by New York Times *bestselling author B.J. Daniels,*
available July 2014, only from Harlequin® Intrigue®.

Copyright © 2014 by Barbara Heinlein

HIEXP69770

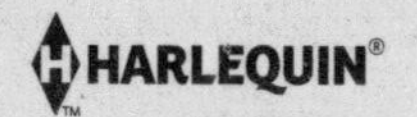

INTRIGUE®

A DEDICATED COP VOWS TO FIND THE MISSING SON OF A HAUNTING BEAUTY IN THE THIRD STORY IN JOANNA WAYNE'S BLOCKBUSTER *BIG "D" DADS* MINISERIES

Dallas homicide detective Travis Dalton came to the city's seediest nightspot to put a deadly criminal mastermind out of business. Instead, he ends up rescuing a woman with haunting eyes he can't forget. But Faith Ashburn isn't what she seems. Her teenage son is missing. And that's just the tip of the iceberg.

For six months, Faith has been searching for her special-needs boy, only to discover he was concealing secrets that could get them both killed. In desperation, she turns to the rugged cowboy cop, who may know more than he's letting on. While she's in Travis's unofficial custody at his family ranch, he vows to protect her, even as the evidence against her son mounts. Now Faith has no choice but to trust this dangerously arousing man who makes her believe in a future she might not live to see....

HARD RIDE TO DRY GULCH

BY JOANNA WAYNE

Only from Harlequin® Intrigue®.
Available July 2014 wherever books and ebooks are sold.

www.Harlequin.com

HI69771

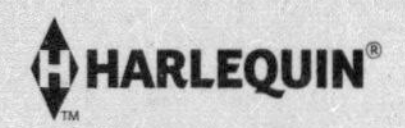

INTRIGUE®

A MAN OF HONOR IN A TOWN WITHOUT ANY...

Erin Barrett was the sole survivor of an armed assault on her company. Her saving grace? Undercover agent Kyle Goodluck, who'd grown from troubled youth to total warrior. Though he'd agreed to protect Erin, he still had unanswered questions. Starting with how much she could be trusted. But only Erin knew what these terrorists wanted—and were willing to kill for. Kyle just had to gauge how forthcoming she was going to be about it. And she'd already proved herself to be a survivor. Standing their ground as New Mexico heated up with crossfire, Kyle wouldn't settle for anything less than absolute victory. But with Erin as his spirit guide, he wouldn't have to settle for anything anymore....

UNDERCOVER WARRIOR

BY AIMÉE THURLO

Only from Harlequin® Intrigue®.
Available July 2014 wherever books and ebooks are sold.

www.Harlequin.com

HI69772R

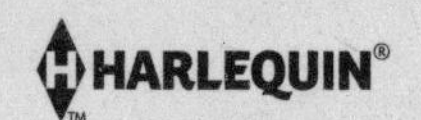

INTRIGUE®

WILL LOVING HER MEAN LEAVING HER?

Bodyguard Logan Payne wants justice for his father's murder. Stacy Kozminski, a gutsy (and gorgeous) jewelry designer, wants revenge for her father's imprisonment. Drawn together by the circumstances and sorrows of their past, they stage an engagement while seeking the truth about their fathers. No one—including Stacy's own thieving brothers—can escape Logan's scrutiny as he tries to protect her from bombs and bullets. But in their pursuit of a killer, Stacy and Logan realize that perhaps their greatest risk comes in loving each other.

EXPLOSIVE ENGAGEMENT

BY LISA CHILDS

Only from Harlequin® Intrigue®.
Available July 2014 wherever books and ebooks are sold.

www.Harlequin.com

HI69773